HIS PACKAGE

PENELOPE BLOOM

1

LILITH

People always thought I wasn't a "people person," whatever that even means. Well, guess what, assholes? I was totally a people person. There were a lot of things I liked about people. I enjoyed watching slightly unfortunate things happen to people who deserved it. I liked making people uncomfortable. Just because frolicking through a grassy field with my best friend and a picnic basket in my hand wasn't my idea of paradise, it didn't make me a psychopath. The fact that I'd probably choose to save a cat's life before a person's life... Well, that admittedly might push me a little farther toward the psychopath end of the spectrum, but nobody's perfect.

Everybody had to find their joys in life. Guilty pleasures. My joys just happened to involve the misfortune of others. Maybe there was a less disturbing way to phrase that... I don't like most people, and I enjoy seeing them suffer? No, still right.

Basically, I assumed pretty much everybody had some bad karma coming their way, and if I was lucky enough to see it happening, it was a bonus. The guy who just spilled coffee on his tie while commuting to work probably walked right past his innocent little golden retriever who just wanted a belly rub a few hours ago. *Karma.* The woman who had a scrap of toilet paper trailing from her heel after lunch break probably gave some poor customer service worker a hard time about her coupon not working the night before. Worse, the reason the coupon didn't work was probably that, like ninety percent of people, she didn't bother reading the details on the back. *Boom.* Karma strikes again.

But there's something I enjoy even more than casual acts of the universe's great balancing act. I don't excite easily, and I don't make a habit of smiling—but I especially enjoy waiting for karma to strike down someone when they've pissed me off.

And that's how it all started.

I lived across the hall from Mr. Perfect. I didn't know his name, even though he'd lived across from me for a few weeks now, and I didn't plan to know it. It was probably something douchey like "Cade," "Tade," or "Spade." Guys like him always had names like that, like they just rolled out of a yacht wearing boat shoes with a sweater wrapped around their hips.

Mr. Perfect didn't dress like that, but you could totally see him pulling it off. Something about the hair or the way he had one of those obnoxious faces that probably would even look good bald. It could've been how you could look at him and practically see the long, unbroken line of absolutely gorgeous people who had to sleep together over the centuries to produce a man with such perfect genetics. Or maybe it was just the stupid way he kept himself in such incredibly good shape—I mean, come on, who needs their body to look like it's classily trying to fight its way out of everything you wear, perfectly shaped muscle by perfectly shaped muscle?

I'd decided, in a very out-of-character moment, to give him a chance the first day he moved in. It's important to note that my decision had almost nothing to do with how good he looked or any bizarre fantasies I might have had about him and my heaving bosoms. It was nothing like that. I just thought I'd be neighborly.

Instead of my usual glare, I just kind of looked his way and waited for him to introduce himself. I even gave him one of those subtle head nods I see guys give each other. I'd seen both the chin tilt up and the chin tilt down variation, so I picked one.

I didn't expect much in return. Maybe a chin tilt or a chin dip. Maybe a smile. Maybe he'd drag me into his room and have his way with me because he'd never seen such an untamed beauty like myself.

But he completely ignored me. Not even eye contact. *Nothing.* So, in the immortal words of the kids back in middle school, "it was on."

He wanted to be perfect? He wanted to practically wear a sign around his neck that says "my life is better than yours?" Fine. He could knock himself out. But if I go out of my way to not glare at you, then you better bet your ass you at least owe me a head nod.

That was mistake number one.

His next mistake was continuing to look like he had some secret stash of Liquid Luck from the Harry Potter universe stashed in his apartment, like every day of his life was a never-ending series of perfectly fortunate coincidences. You could just see it in his eyes.

But the details aren't what matter. What mattered was that he irritated me. So I'd been aggressively waiting for the universe to realize it owed him about thirty years of bad luck all in one moment ever since. I didn't want anything seriously bad to happen to the guy, but it would've made my day if I could just see him fall flat on his face once. I'd even settle for a funny bone injury. Maybe his toilet could back up and flood his apartment with crap. *Anything*, really.

I'd felt like a shadow cast by the glorious ray of light that was his life since the day he'd moved in, and I'd had about enough.

It was a Tuesday, which meant I'd probably run into him before I made it to my apartment. I *may* have had a vague idea of the general time he got back to the apartment complex after work, but it's not like I was a stalker. The man just ran his life like clockwork, and he either got here half an hour early and waited outside until exactly five to come in, or his luck extended to never having a train run late or experiencing traffic. Considering we lived in New York City, I had trouble believing either.

I left my apartment at two till five, not because I wanted to run into him, but because it was when I happened to be leaving my apartment. It took about two minutes to get from the stairs to the mailbox, so he just so happened to be walking in right as I was leaving the stairwell.

He didn't dress flashy. Cheap sunglasses, faded blue t-shirt, and jeans. Of course, he made it all look like a million dollars, which made *me* want to trip him. If karma wasn't going to get the job done, I'd be happy to do some contract work.

The mailboxes for residents were set into the wall and designed for giants. I was a respectable five foot six, but I had to stand on my tiptoes to turn the key on my box and reach inside. Mr. Perfect's box was right next to mine. He had no trouble reaching his while I tried to maintain some dignity on my tiptoes and with my face squished against the wall. I fished out a surprisingly big package from my box.

We both came away from our mailboxes with packages in our hands—mine an unassuming beige box, and his a highly feminine, pink box with a silky white ribbon to keep it closed.

"Nice Package," I said. I was a little surprised to hear my own voice. I thought my brain and my body had agreed on a strict passive-aggressive tactic, but I also wasn't about to apologize for throwing a little snark his way.

He turned to regard me with a raised eyebrow. *God.* The guy was good looking. It was almost sickening, like he wasn't satisfied with "movie-star" level good looks. No, he had to keep climbing the charts until he was perfect. You couldn't even call him so perfect he was boring, because part of his perfection was how he was precisely unique in just the right spots—like his eyebrows that were maybe too dark or too thick, but somehow completely at home on his face. Then there was his nose. I'd never spent any amount of time studying a man's nose before, but it *was* a nice nose. Dignified. Noble, even. It was a nose that made me wonder if I'd somehow been suddenly converted into a "nose person." Was that even a thing?

"Yours is bigger," he said, nodding toward the package in my hands.

There was a playful note in his voice that had me fighting to suppress a grin. I didn't normally have to struggle not to smile. The whole not smiling thing came pretty naturally. I also didn't get nervous around guys, so the weird, uneasy feeling in my stomach must have just been what intensely disliking somebody did to your body.

"Yeah, well, the dildo I ordered was extra large." I gave the box a little tilt and glared at him.

He laughed. It was a deep, rich, sound. "Should I send the paramedics across the hall if you don't come out of your apartment by tomorrow?"

"No," I said. "Send a plumber."

He laughed again, and I caught myself *almost* smiling as I looked up at him and those neatly arranged, white teeth of his. "Don't let me hold you up. Big plans. I get it."

"Yeah, extra large plans," I muttered before I turned and hurried up the stairs. What an asshole. He could pretend to be charming and nice all he wanted, but he'd never so much as introduced himself to me. Only turns on the charm when I talk about huge dildos? Probably a pervert...

I *had* actually ordered a dildo, but it was a normal-sized one, and he didn't need to know any of that. I also didn't subscribe to the idea that owning a respectable sex toy arsenal had any implications about your sex life or lack thereof. You could either have the tools to get the job done on hand, or you'd need to call in somebody to do it for you. Me? I preferred to be prepared.

Once I was back in my apartment, I spent an extra few minutes brutalizing the package because I was too lazy and stubborn to walk five steps to the kitchen for scissors.

I was expecting to find my seven point-two-inch long and two-inch wide date for the evening. Instead, a lame, manilla envelope was sitting there.

I picked it up and turned it over. A couple of plastic cards fell out, but the packet of papers inside got stuck. If this was a new spam mail tactic, it was working, because my curiosity was peaked.

Roosevelt, my cat, was interested too. He was a munchkin breed, which was basically the corgi of the cat world—really short legs on a normal sized body. You could make the argument that it was a little messed up to breed a cat to have stubby, short little legs. If they ever got out in the wild, they'd probably lose a street fight with another cat because they wouldn't have the same reach, or whatever. But you could also make the argument that it was completely awesome.

I picked up one of the cards that had fallen out and narrowed my eyes at the picture. It was my neighbor's driver's license. *Bob Smith?* I guess I was wrong on the whole Cade or Spade naming game, but Bob was almost worse. Maybe there's someone out there named Bob who is super awesome—let's be honest, probably not—but leave it to my neighbor to take a name like Bob and make me question all my previously held stereotypes about the name. *Asshole.*

I tossed the card back down into the box and thought long and hard. Opening someone's mail by mistake was pretty forgivable, I thought. So up until this point, I didn't feel too guilty. If I dug into the papers in the envelope, on the other hand, I might have to start feeling bad. I grunted in annoyance and closed the flaps of the box back up. Whatever secrets *Bob Smith* was holding, I didn't care enough to subject myself the small dose of guilt I'd feel from digging through his mail on purpose.

Someone knocked hard on my door. I scratched Rosevelt under his chin, then went to the door.

I carefully arranged my face before I pulled it open. I was aiming for "you have interrupted something extremely important," but as soon as I saw my neighbor standing in the doorway, my expression went blank.

He was holding a purple dildo that had some really nice, prominent veins worked into the mold. Normally, I would've taken a moment to appreciate and bask in the craftsmanship. Solid mold-work. Nice finish on the silicone, and a great suction-capable base. Everything a girl could dream of. Deep down, I was probably embarrassed, but I learned a long time ago that it was better to own your embarrassment than hiding from it.

"Oh good. You found my date," I said, snagging the dildo from his hand. I emphasized my point by slamming the suction cup on the back of the balls against the door frame where it stuck and then began to wobble menacingly between our eyes.

He watched me with mild amusement. "Your date found his way into my mailbox. I was wondering if you got my package, too?"

"I think I'd know it if I got your package."

He didn't seem to think my pun-work was amusing. His arms were crossed in a way that managed to make his biceps and chest look lickable, though I thought I'd rather bite them. Guys like him had enough pleasure in their lives, after all.

"You're sure?" he asked. There was a tense edge to his voice.

For some reason, his tone made me want to lie about my discovery. Maybe the universe had finally found a way to throw Mr. Perfect a much-deserved curveball. Unless having his parents dub him "Bob Smith" was its one and only attempt at balance. Maybe it saw inside my dark, twisted little heart and knew I was the perfect accomplice.

I crossed my arms right back at him and gave an Academy Award-worthy shrug. "Yeah. Pretty sure. I just got some cat food.

Maybe she didn't have enough space to put both packages in my box, so they shoved my dildo in your hole."

His nostrils flared a little. They were nice nostrils if that was possible, and seeing a little bit of anger on his face only seemed to make him look more untouchably god-like. He had dark hair, a light dusting of stubble, and light gray eyes. His skin was a little pale, but I kind of liked that. It meant he at least didn't prance around outside, flexing his muscles, or worse—donning a banana hammock, greasing up, and sliding into one of those radiation chambers they call tanning beds.

After a long, tense pause, he sighed. "If it turns up, you know where to find me."

"Sure." I flicked the dildo, watched it wobble, and then yanked it free of the door frame with a two-handed grip. It made a vulgar *schlup* noise as I wrenched it free. "Thanks for bringing my date back, by the way."

He sighed again and shut the door. *My door.* What kind of person shuts somebody else's door to end a conversation?

I looked down at the dildo with an angry frown, like it might have the answers for me. I lobbed it even more angrily toward the couch, which unfortunately put Roosevelt in its direct path. He let a frightened little warcry loose as he dove out of the way.

I picked up the thick envelope inside the box one more time, hesitated, and then slid the papers back inside without looking. *Sorry, universe. I don't want to get dragged into this one.*

2

LIAM

I double checked the email on my phone. The package *had* been delivered this afternoon. Either the girl across the hall was lying, or it'd gone in someone else's box. There was no way for me to check unless I wanted to waste the evening sitting in the lobby while I watched every last person check their mail. Even that was pointless because I didn't know what size or type of box I was looking for, or if it had been collected earlier in the day.

None of that mattered.

I knew in my gut that the neighbor girl had it. I couldn't figure out what her deal was. Ever since I'd moved in, she had done nothing but try to glare straight through me. It was like she *knew*--like somehow she saw right through me and the flimsy lies I'd wrapped myself in these past few weeks. It wasn't inconceivable, after all. My step-sister's pettiness had very few limits, and I wouldn't put it past her to bribe random people across the city to keep an eye out for someone matching my description. The neighbor girl could be texting Celia about the package right now, for all I knew.

I sunk down on the edge of my bed and raked my hands

through my hair. I was still waiting for somebody to tell me the last few months had been a bad joke. My step-sister had always been batshit crazy, but her recent antics put everything in our past to shame.

I didn't want to think about it. Any of it.

If I kept laying low, it'd blow over. Fighting back or making a big fuss would only prolong the frustration. If I didn't give her any new ammunition, she'd get bored like she always did, and I could go back to my normal life. No more of these ridiculous distractions or games I'd been forced to play. I'd be free to focus on my company again, though even that idea felt hollow. The company had been my only concern for years now, and having to remove myself from it, even temporarily, was making me start to question why I was sidelining my entire life for my work.

I'd made all the money I could possibly need. I'd achieved the goals I set out to achieve. I was damn good at what I did, and there was no imperative for me to keep striving to be better, yet I felt compelled back to the office, to the grind and the competition. No relationship had ever been able to compete with that compulsion, but every day I spent laying low made me question my dedication even more. Maybe it *was* time to loosen up.

Somebody knocked at my door.

I hurried to the door and found the girl from across the hall standing there, glaring up at me from those eye-liner clad eyes of hers. "Here's your stupid package. Turns out your name was on it. *Whoops.*"

Unsurprisingly, she didn't sound remotely apologetic. There was a kind of deadpan quality to her voice that didn't quite match with the look she had in her eyes—like a constant challenge, a dare of some kind, but whatever the challenge was, I couldn't begin to guess.

My heart sank when I saw the package was ripped open. I didn't dare ask her if she'd read the contents of the envelope, so I tried to stare her down. Most people weren't comfortable with silence, especially when it was combined with eye contact. It was the quickest way to judge the strength of someone's character, in my opinion. So when ten seconds and then twenty went by without her so much as flinching away from my gaze, I decided the tough front she wore may not have been an act after all.

"Thanks." She said in that dry, uninterested way of hers after half a minute had passed. "That's what you say when somebody does something nice for you." She gave the box a hard shove into my stomach and started back toward her door.

"Wait. You didn't look inside?"

"Believe it or not, I don't really care to know what kind of weird shit you get mailed to you."

I pulled out the envelope and saw the seal was broken on the flap. "Then why did you open this?"

Those deep brown eyes of hers flicked away from mine and then back again. It was the first sign of weakness she'd shown, and it helped to know she *was* human beneath the wall of disinterest she was putting up. "Why did you open my dildo box?" she countered.

"I thought it was mine," I said through gritted teeth, even though I knew I was setting myself up for what was about to come.

"Boom," she said, emphasizing the word with a lazy twitch of her eyebrows. "And I thought your stupid envelope was mine. Any more stupid questions?"

I narrowed my eyes. "I don't believe you."

"And I don't care."

I crossed my arms and waited.

"What?" she asked. "You think I'm going to crack just because you want to go all sparkly eyes and silent on me?"

She broke eye contact quickly this time, and she even fidgeted with the hem of her shirt before looking back up at me. Little by little, I was winning the battle of wills, and I found myself enjoying the unspoken contest hidden in our words. I could already tell she wasn't like the women who had failed to hold my interest before. A kind of spark lurked behind those cold eyes of hers, and I'd be lying if I said I wasn't curious about her story. I wanted to know how someone so beautiful ended up so cynical and dark.

She *was* pretty. Porcelain skin and ink-black hair. Her features were soft and feminine with a chin that came to an almost sharp point. She had a personality full of sharp edges, from what I could tell, and it seemed fitting that her face had at least one sharp edge to match.

But the part of her that fascinated me most was her mouth. She seemed to have nearly complete control over her facial expressions, and for whatever reason, she apparently wanted to show the world that she was over it. I could respect that. I knew about hiding myself. I knew about putting on a mask, and not just since my step-sister's bullshit.

But her mask wasn't perfect. Those full lips had a tendency toward twitching at times. To a careless observer, it would look like nothing. To me, it looked like her laugh. When I'd pressed her buttons, there was the hint of a tightness that pulled her features inward. Again, barely noticeable, but as good as a glare to me.

She flipped her hand up by the wrist in a way that said *whatever, I'm over this*, then she turned to leave again.

"Have dinner with me," I said.

She paused just outside her door, which was propped open by a battered book. When she spoke, she didn't even turn to face me. "Why would I do that?"

"Because I think you looked inside my package, and I think maybe you'll tell me the truth if I soften you up with some wine."

"Wine?" She still stood with her hand resting on the door to her apartment, head down slightly. "I only eat raw, bloody meat. So that'll be a hard, 'no' from me."

"Then we'll eat some raw, bloody meat. I don't care. Just say yes."

She moved inside her apartment and finally turned to look at me, but only by sticking her face between the door and frame. It was the first time I'd seen something close to a real smile on her face, but it was a crooked one. "Maybe, but I've actually got plans tonight. Seven inches of them."

She pulled the book out of the door's way, and it swung shut on its own. I was left standing in the hallway, feeling like I'd somehow been outmaneuvered in a game I hadn't agreed to play. *What the hell?*

There was a lurching feeling in my chest, too, almost like I was standing at the edge of a huge cliff and looking down. Was it dread? Anticipation?

I wanted to groan with frustration. All I should have been focused on was keeping my head down and getting through the next couple weeks or even months. However long it took my stepsister to give up. She wanted to sabotage my life and my reputation, so I'd gone incognito. I left behind my apartment, my office, and my normal life. I could still manage my work remotely, even if it was a pain in the ass.

So I had enough on my plate without letting the girl across the hall slide her way into my brain, but that's exactly what she was doing. Maybe I was just so used to women falling at my feet that she had captured my interest from the first hint of resistance she showed. Or maybe she was just my type. More likely, it was a combination of both.

I was looking through my fridge for a beer when it hit me that she'd just admitted she was going back in her apartment to have some fun with the dildo I'd returned to her. The falling, empty feeling in my stomach surged with a wave of heat. The thought of my sarcastic neighbor with a fondness for dark humor getting off was making all the wrong kinds of ideas pop into my head.

It was just the latest ridiculous development in a long line of ridiculous developments, and I was seriously starting to wonder if I'd be better off letting my step-sister win. It was only money and pride, after all. But on the other hand, what else did I have?

3

LILITH

I ripped a sigh from the depths of my soul. For some people, a sigh was a call for help. They wanted the concerned onlooker to lean over and say, "oh, you poor thing, what's wrong?" For me, a sigh was more like a warning shot. It said I was teetering on the edge of tolerance, and I wasn't in the mood to put up with anybody's bullshit. The world was cruel, and I would be too if they tested me.

I was at work. My official job title was "secretary." Four years of college, twenty-five years of rolling my eyes at the idea of demeaning, insulting jobs that put women in archaic, subservient roles to men, *and bam.* Secretary.

I'd really nailed that one.

As it turned out, most of the successful businesswomen I'd admired had badassed their way to the top of their fields through exceptional talent, good luck, or family connections.

I was zero for three. *So far.*

I hadn't ever been the most talented girl in the room, or particularly lucky. And the only family connections I had were some unpleasant memories and weird personality quirks that definitely pointed back to my strange upbringing. One thing I *did* have going for me was a stubborn determination to keep trying, even in the face of impossible odds.

So I was biding my time, instead. Yes, I was sitting outside the office I wanted to ride one day, but I was also using my weekends to get a master's degree in business—a fact I'd never admit, even under torture. I wasn't big on people knowing my personal business. I'd had a childhood full of my parents trying to micro-manage my life. Now that I was on my own, I wasn't about to hand even an ounce of control to anyone else. If they didn't know my dreams, they couldn't try to dictate how I got there.

As far as people went, my boss was kind of okay. That was also something I'd never admit to his face. I'd end up being the one who had to call a contracting company to get all the door-ways in the building enlarged to fit his swollen head if I ever complimented him. Sometimes I thought he was just too clueless to be anything but supremely self-confident, and other times I thought maybe he was actually some kind of evil genius under-neath the often bumbling, easy-going exterior.

He busted out of his office like Kramer from *Seinfeld* as if the mere thought of him summoned him up.

William Chamberson.

He and his twin brother, Bruce, owned Galleon Enterprises, and I had the misfortune of working as his... *whatever I was.* God knew he hardly used me for normal secretary work. If anything, I was his anti-secretary. Instead of helping people get in contact with him and setting up meetings, I was supposed to help him avoid everyone and all meetings. He even seemed to encourage laziness and my indifferent attitude at work.

William and his brother were both married, but it didn't stop every single woman in the very large company from openly talking about how badly they wish they could have some alone time with the men. Opinions were pretty split on which one was the most popular target. Women who were more buttoned-up and "Type A" seemed to lust after Bruce and his matter-of-fact, borderline-obsessive hunt for perfection in all things. The "Type B" women liked William and his wild, unpredictable personality.

I thought they were all idiots. William and his brother were entertaining, but complete mental-cases.

William opened his mouth to speak, but the phone rang.

Both our eyes went to it. It was a sleek, fancy, charcoal-colored phone with a lot of buttons I still hadn't quite figured out in my four years of working here.

"Going to get that?" he asked.

"No. I cleaned all the fingerprints off it this morning."

"Right," he said. He took two long-legged steps to my desk and leaned forward with a conspiratorial look on his face. He picked up the phone and set it back down to silence the ringing, which also left a fresh set of prints on it. "Listen. I've got a favor to ask. I know you're not big on the whole *work* thing. But I'll give you whatever you want if you can just man the fort tonight. It's a company party, and I need an inside man to tell me if this jerk I knew in high school shows up. I might've fired off a few tweets in his direction last night, and things got a bit out of hand."

"Sorry. No penis. Look elsewhere."

"*Inside woman*, whatever. It's a part of speech. Phrase of speech? Shit. What's the thing you call those things?"

I spread my palms. "Not sure. You didn't hire me for my mastery of English and grammar."

"Yeah, what did I hire you for again? I keep forgetting."

"I ignore the people who try to talk to you, so you don't have to talk to them."

He patted my head twice and smiled. "And you're a good girl for that."

I slapped his hand away and gave a little warning curl of my lip.

He grinned. "You're kind of like the angry dog I chain up in front of the house. It makes me look more intimidating."

"Yeah, because I'm so terrifying."

"Well," he said carefully. "If you don't want to have your soul sucked out through your eyes, or some kind of Pagan ritual performed over your bed while you sleep, you kind of *are* terrifying. But in the best possible way."

I locked eyes with him and didn't blink.

He nodded his head and pointed at me. "See? That's exactly what I'm talking about. Yep. So, tonight? Can you do it? I'll give you, I don't know, what's a reasonable amount of money for three hours of extra work? A thousand dollars?"

"More like ten."

"Okay, whatever. Ten, then. Can you do it?"

I sighed. "Ten thousand dollars is *not* a reasonable amount of money for three hours of work. I'll do it for my normal pay, but only because you said I was scary. *Shit.* Wait..." I looked up at the ceiling and tried to decide if I really wanted to say what I was about to say. I thought of the way my heart pounded when Mr. Perfect had asked me to go to dinner with him, and I knew I couldn't resist. "There's actually one catch. I might have agreed to a date tonight. I mean, I said 'maybe,' but I was thinking of changing it to 'yes.' He promised me raw meat," I added as if that explained everything.

William took a step back and held his mouth open in a stupid "O" shape that *should have* looked ridiculous, but the man had been blessed by all that was unfair with perfect features, so he still looked good.

"A date? My Lilith? A date? Oh my God. What are we going to wear? I've got to call the wife. Hailey needs to know about this. Is this a makeover scenario? Definitely, right? No, wait, is he... is the guy... *like you?*"

"What do you mean *like me?*"

"You know," he said, gesturing at his clothes and making a strange, constipated face. "Kind of, well, the way you are. You're very special," he said finally, as if he'd found the perfect way to express it.

"He's not like me, no," I said. "He's more like your brother, maybe."

William spontaneously gagged. It actually sounded convincing enough that I wasn't sure it was staged. "Bruce? You agreed to a date with an OCD, telephone pole up the ass, horrible sense of humor, worst half of a pair of twins kind of guy?"

"No. I mean, I don't really know what's up his ass, I didn't look, *yet*. And I just mean he's more like Bruce in that he's actually kind of serious. And I hardly know him. My dildo got delivered to his mailbox, and I got his package in mine. So he invited me to eat. Or dinner. Or whatever."

William crossed his arms and pinched his chin as he paced a small, restless circle like he was in the middle of uncovering some grand mystery. "First thing's first, Lilith. The next time you talk to me about any of your disgusting sex toy hobbies, you're fired. I don't need to know what kind of devil spawn you shove up your hoo-hah, okay?"

"Seven point two inches," I said slowly. "Purple. Thick veins—"

"Stop!" He shook his head and pressed his fingers to his temples. "More importantly, there's a premium opportunity for innuendo here. You realize that, right? His *package* in your *box*? You could even say he—"

"Already covered all that," I sighed.

He looked a little irritated but recovered quickly. "I don't get it though. How does him getting your dildo in the mail lead to him asking you on a date?"

"Maybe I charmed him? Or maybe he thought I was pretty."

William laughed. "It just doesn't make sense," he said as if I hadn't even spoken. "Serial killer? That's always the first thing you have to worry about as a woman, right?"

"Totally. Maybe if he's a serial killer, he and I can compare notes. Save electricity by using the same freezer for body storage."

William narrowed his eyes. "The scary part is I don't even know if that's a joke. And I don't want to, because if I knew the truth, I'd probably be next on your list."

"Maybe you already are."

He ignored my threat. William had known me long enough to learn that I was more bark than bite, but at least he knew to still be afraid of my bad moods. "One thing is obvious. We need to know more about this so-called "man." Habits. Schedule. Mannerisms. Hobbies. Work. We need to know it all, and fast. I can't have you going on a date with him until we know more."

"Damn. If only there was some obvious, easy way to quickly find out about somebody. Like... some ancient social custom where you maybe share a meal and a few hours, talk about yourselves, and that kind of thing."

"Forget the hypotheticals, Lilith. I know what we have to do. Hold on."

He disappeared into his office. When he came back a few minutes later, he was holding a pair of high-tech goggles, some balled-up black clothing, and something that looked kind of like a megaphone, but with a clear, plastic bowl and a microphone in the middle. He set it down on the desk in front of me.

"This is the plan. You use all this awesome shit. You spy on him. If he's a creep, you say no. If he's normal, you do the date. I'll hold the job open for you tonight, just in case." He tapped my desk twice with his finger and winked. "You're welcome."

"Do I get to ask why you have all this?"

"No, because explaining would require me to tell you intimate details about the wonderful, robust sex life I have with my lovely wife."

"I'll promise never to talk about dildos again if you promise to never talk about your 'robust' sex life. Ever again."

"Deal."

I shook my head at all the equipment. "Did you at least, I don't know, sanitize it all?"

"Of course we did. What kind of barbarians do you think we are?"

"This is a new low, William. Even for you. Do you seriously think I'm going to go full-blown stalker on this guy just so I have an excuse to use some cool gadgets?" I ran my finger along the sleek and shiny night vision goggles. "Even if they are really cool high-tech gadgets. What do you think I am, twelve?"

4

LIAM

I grabbed a coffee from the barista and did a quick, casual glance around the cafe before I moved to sit with my business partners, Price and Kade.

"You call this 'dressing inconspicuously?'" I asked as I sat down.

Price pulled out the collar on his Hawaiian shirt and looked offended. "This is how people on vacation dress. I'm a tourist."

Price was my half-brother, and we both had my dad's sharp features, along with the broad shoulders and long legs. After that, the similarities stopped. My hair was dark, and his was dirty blond like his mother's. My eyes were gray, and his were light brown.

Kade was a mountain of a man who had, oddly enough, started as an intern with the company a few years ago. You wouldn't believe it from looking at him. He looked like he'd maybe just walked through a few walls, glared at somebody in charge, and dared someone to tell him he wasn't a co-owner of the business. He had a *slight* criminal background, but I tried not to dwell too much on that.

Kade was wearing a t-shirt that stretched to fit his frame and a pair of sweatpants along with a black ball-cap and glasses.

I snatched the glasses off his face and pulled the hat off. "Trying too hard not to get noticed makes you noticeable," I said. I looked at Price and could only shake my head. "And that's not how tourists in *New York City* dress. They wear "I Love New York" shirts or something. Besides, dressing like a New Yorker is a lot less noticeable than dressing like a tourist, dumbass."

Kade only shrugged, but Price wore a sour expression.

"Maybe I'm a tourist *from* Florida. Ever think of that, genius?" Price asked.

"Can we just get to business?" I took another look over my shoulder, though I wasn't sure what I expected to see, anyway. If Celia did have somebody following me, I doubted they'd be wearing a trenchcoat, fedora, and pretending to read a newspaper. It could have been any one of the dozens of people sipping coffees, working on laptops, or eating bagels.

"How long are we going to keep this up?" Kade asked. He had a deep voice, like boulders rubbing against each other.

"Until I know she's done fucking with me."

"I could try talking to her again," Price suggested. "She *is* my sister, even if she kind of hates me."

My father decided to make my family tree as confusing as possible by having me with his first wife, remarrying when I was two and having Price with his second wife, who already had a daughter from a previous marriage. In the end, I wound up with Price, my half-brother, and Celia, my step-sister, who was also Price's sister.

We'd all grown up together from a young age, and from as early as I could remember, Celia had always taken an unhealthy interest in me. We were almost exactly the same age, which meant I couldn't escape her all throughout school.

"She *kind of* hates you like I kind of hate wrinkles in my socks," Kade said to Price.

I stared at him. "What?"

"You know," he said. "When you get that fold in your socks, and it feels like a little lump under your foot all day. It's the worst."

"Did it ever occur to you that you could just take off the shoe and fix it?" I asked.

"Plus, the way you phrased that, it was like you were going to one-up it." Price added. "Like, I don't know, 'she kind of hates you like I kind of hate getting stabbed.' That kind of thing." Kade looked at Price like he was an idiot. "What kind of person only kind of hates getting stabbed? That's something you *all the way* hate."

Price gave me a helpless look. I shrugged. Kade was great at what he did for the company, but making jokes was not one of his strong suits.

Our company sold investment packages to big-time financial advisors and even hedge fund managers. Normally, the advisors and managers put together their own investment packages, but that was our spin on the industry. We did it better, and we had the data to prove it. Their clients were happier, and we just took a small cut, so everyone was happy.

Instead of taking percentages and incentives, we put together the cutting edge portfolios month-by-month and sold them for a premium. We had one of the best records in the business, and it was only getting better. I'd always had a nose for stocks, and that was where my contribution to the company came in. I put together the packages every month, and I busted my ass researching every possible option. Most portfolios promised five or seven percent returns, but we aimed for ten. It wasn't easy, but I liked the challenge, and I'd rarely had a bad month since we started.

Price was our salesman. He needed a lot of structure and guidance to stay focused on work, but when he was paying atten-tion, he could sell air to a fish. Kade, despite looking the way he did, was basically a genius when it came to software design. He had taken what I did and turned it into an intuitive program that we could sell as a monthly service. I made the selections, and all our clients had to do was stay subscribed to get fed each month's new package of premium stock selections.

Together, we made a pretty damn good team.

I handed a USB drive to Kade. "This is for January." I looked to Price. "Don't make any promises if you don't have to, but I'm pretty confident this package is going to pull twelve, maybe even fourteen percent."

Price whistled. "Maybe we should get my sister to chase you into hiding more often."

I groaned. "We still haven't seen if all the damage she did before I started laying low will come back to bite us."

"I think you're giving her too much credit," Price said. "So she spread some bullshit rumors and got a few magazines to write smear articles about you. So anybody who pays attention thinks you're a sex-crazed, BDSM-fiend who can't keep his dick in his pants. You're gay. You're all the things. *So what?* Maybe we'll bring in some female clients who are hoping to get a piece of that. We could start making you wear a collar with spikes or something. You know, play it up."

"You think that's where it was going to stop? Celia wants to see me in ruins. In her screwed up head, I wronged her, and she's not going to stop until she thinks she's won. *Or,* until she gets bored, which is what I'm aiming for."

"I still can't believe she wanted to have an affair with you." Price grinned, then his eyes sank to the table, and he looked like he was about to gag. "Okay, actually I can completely believe it. I'm just surprised she finally came out and said it like that."

"They're not biologically related," Kade said. "They could have perfectly healthy children. I don't see the problem."

"The problem, number one, is she's married," I said. "Number two is she's my goddamn step-sister, so it's disgusting. Number three is even if she was single and had no relations to me, I still wouldn't be interested. I've never met a person as naturally evil as Celia. My dick would probably turn black and fall off if it got anywhere near her. No offense, Price."

"None taken. Totally agree with the whole keeping your dick away from her thing, just as a general precaution."

"I think she's pretty," Kade shrugged.

Price punched his shoulder. "That's my sister."

"Sorry. I think your sister's pretty."

"Anything I need to know about?" I interrupted. "On the business side of things, I mean."

Price pursed his lips and shook his head. "Other than the fact that I'm carrying the business while you're sneaking around with a tinfoil hat on? No."

"I think somebody is watching us," Kade said.

I jerked around in my seat and spotted her immediately. The neighbor girl was standing at the entrance to the cafe with a startled look on her face. She was staring right at us.

"I'll handle this," I said, standing.

"You sure you don't want some help? She's cute," Price asked.

I ignored them and headed for the girl.

She did a military-style about-face, turning on her heel before fast-walking out to the sidewalk. If my heart wasn't slamming against my ribs because I thought she *had* been spying on me for Celia all along, the sight of her fast-walk might have been comical.

I had to shove my way through a family coming into the cafe and then fight against the crowd outside, but I was thankfully tall enough to keep an eye on her as she darted down into the subway.

I caught her just before the turnstiles.

"Hey," I said, gripping her shoulder and turning her around to face me. "You want to tell me why you're following me?"

"I wasn't." Her lips were pressed into a thin line as she glared up at me with those defiant eyes of hers.

"You just happened to be there? At a random coffee shop on the opposite end of the city?"

"Yes."

I sighed. "And what's all this, then?" I tugged at the Army green bag she was carrying that looked stuffed to the brim.

She jerked it away from me, glaring. "It's girl stuff. And you shouldn't touch people's things."

I leaned in a little closer. There was a spark of fire in her eyes that was at odds with the way she kept acting like she wanted nothing to do with me. She *had* tracked me down. She *had* followed me. I wasn't buying her story, and I didn't know that I even wanted to. What I wanted was to know more about her. There was a story behind the dark-haired girl who hid her smile, and I was greedy for it. Even if it turned out that she was bought and paid for by my step-sister, I needed to know.

Bringing my face closer to hers made her inch backward until she had her back against a turnstile and people were grumbling angrily as they had to move around us. I got my first real taste of her scent, and it was an enticing one. She smelled sweet as flowers.

The hair on my neck stood up.

"I shouldn't touch people's things? As I recall, you started it."

"It was an accident," she said. The characteristic bite in her words was muted now.

"Accident or not, you touched my package, and now I can't just let you walk away."

The corner of her mouth twitched in that way of hers—a smile. I liked that it was a private language. It was a language few would understand, and it made me feel even more drawn in. "How do you plan to stop me, *Bob*?"

It felt like a cold hand slid its fingers around my heart and squeezed. *Bob.* So she had looked inside the envelope, after all.

There was an edge to the way she said the name, too, like she knew it was an alias—or was I imagining that?

"Seduction," I said. "Maybe. But I'm still trying to figure out if you can be seduced by anything but seven inches of silicone."

"Seven point two," she corrected. "And I guess you'll have to keep trying if you want to know. Won't you?" She emphasized her point with a subtle wiggle of her eyebrows and then pushed me back with a fingertip against my chest. She slid a card from her jacket pocket and scanned it at the turnstile, which rotated and let her through.

"Why the long face?" she asked. "You don't ride the subway? No card?"

I pulled my own card out and scanned it. I stepped right back inside her personal space and grinned down at her. "Was that as far as your plan for avoiding me went? Because you don't stand a chance if that's all you have up your sleeve."

"Well, this is just awkward now. That was supposed to be my smooth exit."

"Can't say that I'm sorry."

She tried to adjust her bag on her shoulder, but the clasp clicked open and sent the contents of her bag spilling to the ground.

"*Shit*," She muttered as she knelt down and started trying to scoop everything back inside.

I bent down to help her and immediately noticed a bulky piece of high tech gear. I held it up and gave her a questioning look. "What the hell are these? Night Vision goggles?"

"I'm a birdwatcher," she said, snatching them from me and shoving them in the bag.

"A listening device?" I asked, holding up another gadget.

"Birds sing," she said in a *duh* kind of way.

"What's your favorite breed of bird?" I asked.

She paused, and I thought I had her, but then she shook her head like I'd said something stupid. "Australian wedge-tailed eagles. They make Bald Eagles look like sissies. A wedge-tail will attack you if you're paragliding. They'll prey on kangaroos. Probably could eat a baby in one bite. They are badasses, basically."

"Where do you even learn something like that?"

She patted her bag. "Bird watching."

I sighed. As much as I wanted to call her on her bluff, I wasn't even sure anymore. Maybe I was letting the throbbing pressure between my legs blind me to the obvious, but I didn't think she was actually working with Celia. Maybe I just didn't want to think she was.

"What about dinner? Is that still a maybe?"

"I guess I could let you take me to dinner. If you're into that kind of thing."

I raised an eyebrow. "Aren't most people into eating?"

"Whatever," she said, but she couldn't hide the way her lips were practically itching to smile. "But not tonight. I have this stupid thing for work. Tomorrow."

Smiling didn't usually come easily to me, but around her, I had to stop myself from grinning like an idiot half the time. Even the way she said, "whatever" was endearing. She tried to make it sound disinterested, but the curve at the corner of her mouth and the sparkle in her eyes gave it an entirely different meaning. It was playful. More and more, I was understanding her language, and I was learning she was nothing like she seemed.

All the sarcasm and dry words were her own kind of game, like a test, even.

"Deal. But I need to know your name if I'm going to be taking you to dinner. You can at least give me that much, right?"

"Lilith."

I pursed my lips and nodded. "Somehow that fits you."

"It fits me just like Bob doesn't fit you."

I tried to brush her comment off with a shrug. "We don't get to pick our names."

"No," she said, eyes never leaving mine. "Most of us don't."

5

LILITH

I leaned against the reception desk at Galleon. The party was being held on one of the upper floors. I was a glorified greeter as people came in on the ground floor. William at least knew me well enough to know I wasn't about to be smiling and saying nice things to everyone who came in. He did mention something about "directing guests to the party," which meant telling them what button to press when they got in the elevator, but I didn't want to rob the poor little guy who had to sit in the elevator and wear a silly hat of his purpose. Instead, I kicked my feet up and killed time on my phone while pretending people weren't giving me dirty looks.

One of my go-to activities on my phone was browsing Reddit, which meant I'd just stumbled across the whole wedge-tailed eagle factoid a few hours before I had to pull that shining nugget of bullshit out of my ass in the subway station earlier. Bob had seemed to buy the excuse, even if it looked like he grudgingly accepted it.

It's not like I was going to use the goggles or the listening thing, anyway. Probably not, at least. I was just bored, and I happened to have been kind of hanging out in the lobby of our apartment when he left, and I maybe happened to be standing in a space where I knew he wouldn't see me as he left.

My excuses rang hollow even in my own head. Right in the center of my brain, there was a muscular, six-foot-three shape, and I was perfectly happy to keep pretending it wasn't there, along with the other piles of repressed memories I carefully avoided. Over time, my brain had become like a hoarder's room that I had to try to navigate blind. Occasionally, I'd bump into an unpleasant memory or a traumatic conversation, but for the most part, I kept my distance. It was easier that way.

A couple walked up to the desk. The guy was wearing a suit, and the woman wore a long black dress covered in what looked like iridescent fish scale patterns. It was kind of cool, but the couple was looking at me like they expected me to get up and kiss their rings, so I looked back to my phone and made a point of ignoring them.

"We're here for the party. We're friends of Bruce Chamberson."

"Cool. The party is across the street. If the door's locked, just knock and wait."

"Across the street?" The man turned around and gestured to all the people who were funneling through the doors and toward the elevators. "Then what are all of these people doing?"

"They're here for the free colon exams. Thirty-sixth floor, if you're interested. You were supposed to bring your own lube, though. Did you—"

The couple was already storming out of the building. *Whoops.* Some people couldn't take a joke.

I knew I was supposed to be keeping an eye out for William's old high school friend, but he had neglected to tell me that apparently, they'd invited hundreds of people to the party. I don't know how I was supposed to spot somebody with "close together eyes like a ferret and a neck that looked like a wet noodle." What the hell did that even mean, anyway?

Only a few minutes had passed when a girl around my age planted her palms on the desk. "Excuse me," she said.

I glanced up at her with a carefully practiced sigh. It was supposed to scare off social predators the same way a lion's roar let everybody know a badass was on the prairie. Unfortunately, the girl seemed unfazed.

She had dark black hair pulled back into a long, ponytail and a pretty badass widow's peak. She was pretty, in an evil villain kind of way, and she was rocking the emerald green dress she wore. I decided to give her my attention.

"Excuse you for what?"

"For interrupting. I can see you're busy, but I was wondering if I could hide out behind the desk just for a few minutes? There's this guy who is kind of bothering me, and I—"

"Go ahead. Just don't touch anything," I said. "And if your nose whistles when you breathe, you're getting kicked out. Fair warning."

She thanked me and hurried around behind the desk to duck beside my chair. I went back to my phone while I waited for the night to end, but the new girl apparently was a talker.

"You work for Galleon, right?" she asked.

"No. I'm homeless. I stole these clothes from a girl I beat and hid in the bathroom."

She grinned. "Sarcasm. I'd almost forgotten what it sounded like. The people I've been hanging around are too tight-assed to even have a sarcastic thought, let alone make a joke."

I *wanted* to say something snarky just to get her to stop talking, but I admittedly felt a little bad for her. She'd apparently had a rough night, and I figured I could act like a normal human, maybe for a few minutes. I may have had a bit of a twisted outlook on social interactions, but I still hadn't figured out a way to turn off my capacity for empathy. *Unfortunately.*

"You said a guy was bothering you? Want me to tase him if he comes in?"

"You have a taser?" she asked.

I dug in my purse and pulled out the device. It was about the size of a deck of cards, and when I squeezed the trigger, arcs of electricity clicked between the metal nodes at the top. The sound was like metal balls clacking together. A few guests heading for the elevators shied away and then started walking faster.

She nodded approvingly. "As long as you tase him between the legs, then yes."

"Where else would you tase somebody?"

She smiled. "The nipple or the asshole, maybe?"

"Damn," I said. I turned to face her. "I think I might actually like you."

"Likewise. I'm Claire." She reached up to shake my hand.

"Lilith."

I thought I saw something strange flash across her eyes, almost like triumph, but I dismissed the idea. It wouldn't make sense, and I wasn't great at reading people, anyway.

William came rushing out of one of the elevators. His hair was a mess and he looked like he had a rapidly forming black eye. Claire ducked a little farther under the counter and pressed a finger to her lips at me.

"I've seen that before," I said, pointing to his eye. "It's one of those African bugs. The ones that lay eggs under your skin. I think you have like three days before flies start bursting out of your face."

He groaned and pressed his palm to the spot with a wince. "Unless African bugs have creepy, pedophile mustaches and are built like Russian heavyweight champions, I don't think so."

"Wow," I said dryly. "Somebody punched you? I can't imagine why anyone would ever think of hitting you, or why they would stop at one punch."

"Not in the mood for your lame jokes, Lilith." He leaned over the desk. "Coincidentally, it was the guy I told you to watch out for."

"So he has a wet noodle neck *and* a Russian heavyweight champion build? I'm having trouble picturing the combination, sorry."

"Whatever, maybe he wasn't *that big*. He caught me by surprise is all. Sucker punch. It's fine. I put some crab meat in his coat pocket, one of the little ones on the inside no one ever uses. Give it a couple days and he's going to be wondering what the hell smells. Bonus points if he throws it in a closet and forgets a few weeks."

"You were carrying around crab meat because..."

"I wasn't. I made a comment. He punched me. I grabbed some food from the buffet, found the coat rooms, and bribed the guy to tell me which coat was his. Any more questions?"

"Is this going somewhere?"

"I mean, a normal person would apologize for letting that thug up without warning me. That was kind of the *one* job I gave you."

"I'm sorry I let a Russian, wet-noodle necked thug punch you in the face."

"That's all I was looking for. Now, are you going to introduce me to the woman hiding under your desk, or do I need to do it myself?"

Claire stood up with surprising grace and brushed off the back of her dress before reaching to shake William's hand. "I'm Claire."

"William," he said. "Do I know you from somewhere?"

"I get that a lot." She laughed a little nervously. "I should really get going, but hey," she turned to grab a post-it note and a pen. She scribbled down her phone number and stuck it to my forehead with a grin. "We should grab coffee sometime."

I peeled the note from my forehead and stuck it on the desk with no intentions of ever calling her again. I had a cat with ridiculous, stubby little legs. What did I need friends for? Besides, I *had* a best friend. She just wasn't exactly in the country for a couple of years. But I had time.

"Let me help you out," William said to Claire. He grabbed another post-it note and wrote down my number. He handed it to Claire with a wink. "Trust me. This one will never call you. You have to win her over by brute force. Can't say the payoff is really worth the work though. The kid practically loves me now, and sometimes I wonder why I bothered getting her to—"

"You're a moron."

He looked at Claire like I'd just professed my love for him. "See what I mean?"

Claire looked at the note and smiled. "Well, thank you. It was nice to meet you. Both of you," she added before leaving.

William made a face after she left. "I swear I know her from somewhere."

"Don't stare too hard or I'll tell Hailey."

"Hailey is comfortable enough in our marriage that I can look at other women. Besides, looking at other women just reminds me how much hotter Hailey is. Take you, for example..."

"Careful," I said. "A few more poorly chosen words out of you and you'll be hanging in my meat-locker."

"Why does that sound vaguely sexual? I think I'm going to gag."

"Maybe because you have the sense of humor of a middle school boy and everything sounds sexual to you?"

"Entirely possible, yeah. Anyway, if you didn't get pissed off so easily, it wouldn't be as fun to mess with you. You bring it on yourself."

"And I only work for you because I eventually plan to overthrow you and build an empire out of your bones."

He nodded appreciatively. "I like the ambition. You keep that up and you might go somewhere."

"Speaking of going somewhere. Can I leave now since I already screwed up the dumb job you gave me?"

"Go, little one. I'm sure you have some Black Arts to practice, or maybe a seance to perform."

I sighed. "Sometimes I wish I really did all these twisted things you think because I'd absolutely put a curse on you. Maybe one that put your dick on your forehead, for starters."

He rolled his eyes. "Har, har. Dickhead. Yeah, that'd be such a knee slapper."

"No, just so you'd have balls in your eyes all day."

I SPENT THE REST OF THE NIGHT CRAMMING FOR A BUSINESS FINAL I had in a couple of days. Most of my classwork was online work, which was a big plus. I'm sure if I told William what I was doing, he'd give me time off. He'd probably even let me off the hook with a lame joke or two, and then he'd forget about the entire thing in a day. But there was the off chance that he'd get all weird and say he was proud or something. *That* was enough to keep me from telling him.

Worse, he might have some kind of connection and secretly arrange for a perfect job opportunity to open up for me. I wanted my badass business career to mean *I* had worked my ass off and earned it. I didn't want it to be a handout.

I must have dozed off because I stirred awake and found a string of drool connecting my face to my desk. I heard the sound of a doorknob shaking across the hall and muttered cursing. I wiped the sleep from my eyes and stumbled toward my door. I opened it quietly and peeked through the crack to see what was going on.

Bob was standing in front of his door with his hands on his hips, and he looked pissed.

"Having a talk with your door?" I asked.

He turned sharply, and for a second, his eyes looked wild, like he thought he was about to have to defend himself. He relaxed when he saw it was me.

"My key apparently doesn't work anymore."

I stepped into the hallway and stuck my hand out. "Give it here. I've lived here long enough to know all the tricks with these stupid locks. Miss Lindsey is too cheap to get new keys, so they all eventually grind down to nubs like this. I'll—"

My stomach sank when I heard my door click shut behind me. *Shit.* A few months ago, it had decided to become a self-closing door, and I'd had to develop a habit of jamming something in the doorframe so I wouldn't get locked out without my keys. Apparently, *Bob Smith* had a mild brain-numbing effect on me.

I tried the handle on my door. Of course, it was locked. One of the extra latches inside *also* had a tendency of swinging into the locked position if the door closed too hard.

"Locked out? That makes two of us," he said.

I sighed. "You're not locked out. You just don't know how to work your key. Give it."

He looked skeptical but handed me the key. I stole a quick look at him and saw he was wearing a sweat-stained t-shirt and shorts. His body was still a little slick with sweat, too.

"Why are you all gross?" I asked as I slid the key into the lock.

"I was working out."

"In the middle of the night?"

"I like the gym when it's empty."

I pushed the key up a little, testing with different amounts of pressure as I carefully tried the doorknob. I found the sweet spot eventually and got the door open.

"Tada," I said. "Now you can go take the shower you desperately need."

He looked down at me as he took the keys, and I could practically *see* his thoughts churning.

I realized how close we were standing as he pinned me in his doorway, and I could smell him. I expected it to be a bad smell, but I should've known better. Somehow, he managed to actually smell all good and manly even though he was drenched in sweat. I'd never been a sweaty-guy kind of girl, but I could feel myself being converted every time a drip of perspiration decided to roll down his clavicle and disappear toward that hard, sculpted chest of his.

My mind flashed with images of fingertips scraping paths across sweaty, muscular skin lit only by what little moonlight filtered in through the windows. I imagined being enveloped by that manly scent that was washing over me like a drug.

"I'm supposed to leave you out here by yourself in the middle of the night after you rescue me?" he asked.

"I can go bug Miss Lindsey for the master key."

"No, you can't. She's out of town until next week. Remember?"

"I can call a locksmith," I said.

"It'll be a few hours at this time of night."

"If you want to invite me inside your apartment so bad, just do it, asshole."

He crossed his arms and leaned against the doorframe with a grin. "What's the deal with you, anyway?"

"Right now? You're the deal with me. If you knew how to work a key, I wouldn't be trapped in the hallway with my stinky, sweaty neighbor."

"Stinky?" he asked. He moved a little closer, still wearing that grin. "You must like stinky, then, if the look on your face is any indication."

I took a step back and shook my head. "If I look happy, it's just because I was fantasizing about kneeing you in the balls."

He grinned, and I had no doubt he could see straight through my lie. "So you admit you *were* fantasizing about my balls?"

"And their destruction, yes."

"Somehow, I think if you got your hands between my legs, you'd have other ideas."

"And somehow, I think you must normally get away with talking to people like that."

"Like what?"

"Like you're so cocksure and confident, like you can just... *assume* everybody you meet wants to choke your sausage."

He chuckled, but his eyes held the fiery smolder as they bore through me. "I don't assume everybody wants to fuck me. Just the ones who look at me like *that.*"

I tried to picture my dad's face on Bob's body instead of the obnoxiously well-crafted spectacle he called a head.

Bob's eyebrows shot up and he flashed a crooked smile. "Okay. I give. That's not the face of somebody who is looking to get lucky, but since I smell so bad, I'd better hop in the shower. I'm not letting you wait out in the hallway in the middle of the night. It's not safe. Come sit on the couch. You can grab a snack or a beer out of the fridge."

"Yeah, because if I stay out here some strange, perverted man might try to kidnap me and take me into his apartment. But if I come with you, I can skip the guesswork, right?"

He licked his lips and barely held a smile at bay. "I think I like you."

"I think you like yourself more."

He laughed. "Do you ever let that mouth of yours rest? *Not that I would,*" he said quietly, eyes drifting down my face to my mouth.

I felt my resistance start to crumble. There was only so much open flirtation I could fight before some of it slipped through the cracks and warmed my chest. I knew there was some snarky, sarcastic remark floating around in my brain, but the only thing I could find was a noncommittal grunt. I swallowed hard, then muttered something about being able to handle myself in a hallway for a few hours.

"I'm sure you can, but all the same. Come on." He gestured for me to step inside.

I didn't plan to obey him but found my feet moving anyway. Before I knew it, I was inside, and it very much felt as though I'd crossed an invisible threshold—one that I'd been fighting the desire to cross since long before I met Bob.

People occasionally tried to get close to me. I pushed back. Sometimes, they tried harder, but I always won. I always managed to scare them off with enough sarcasm or enough snark. Tonight, I'd let Bob win. The worst part was instead of feeling angry about losing, I only felt a little warm and fuzzy.

His apartment was tidy and minimalistic. There were hardly any decorations except a random picture of a rowboat in the hallway that almost looked like a leftover from the previous tenant. Just the bare-bones necessities. "I still think it's more dangerous in here than in the hallway, for the record," I said.

He tilted his head as those grey eyes of his took me in from head to toe. "I'm sure it is, for both of us, but it's a totally different kind of danger."

"What do you mean, do you have pet snakes or something? Or worse, a chimpanzee? People think they're cute until they spend years dressing them like humans. One day your little pseudo-human wakes up, decides he wanted more milk in his cornflakes, and rips your face off. True story."

He laughed. "No snakes or pseudo-humans." He looked like he was deciding whether to say something, then decided against it. "Just make yourself comfortable. I'll be back in a few minutes."

He started peeling his shirt off before he was completely behind the door to the bathroom, and for a split second, I saw every tantalizing inch of his broad, muscular back. I cleared my throat and plopped down on the couch, then immediately got back up to look at myself in a mirror by the entrance.

The shower turned on, and I had to do mental gymnastics to avoid picturing him stripping out of the rest of his clothes as steam billowed around his powerful, sculpted—

I blew out a long, controlled breath. I wasn't even sure why I was fighting my attraction to him so much. I didn't like *people* generally speaking, but I had nothing against penises. Couldn't I just call it sexual infatuation? I didn't have to pretend to like *him*. Maybe I could just imagine he had come in a six-foot-three, silky pink package—the latest model of dildo, complete with a rich bastard attached.

I ran a hand through my hair and leaned back into the couch, sinking deeper. Who was I kidding? I liked the man attached to the penis, too. I liked that he didn't flinch away from the worst I could give. I liked the way he looked at me. I liked that he seemed like the kind of guy who wouldn't even give me a second thought, but he looked at me like I was the only person in the world. Yes, he was pretty obviously hiding something. Yes, he'd probably had the world handed to him on a silver platter, and the idea of giving myself to him as easily as everything else irked me, but I liked him.

He had an air of mystery around him. He carried himself with supreme confidence like he'd already conquered the world and didn't have anything left to prove. Then there were conflicting moments of paranoia that didn't mesh with the confidence he wore so well. There was the package, obviously, and the oddness of having your driver's license mailed to you inside an unmarked manila envelope. There was the way he'd chased me down when he caught me watching him and his equally mysterious friends. And there was even the way he'd jumped like he'd been caught doing something wrong when I found him outside his apartment a few minutes ago.

Bob Smith, if that was even his real name, was absolutely hiding something.

I heard a thump from inside the shower and was jolted back to reality. I fumbled for my phone for a few seconds before realizing I didn't even have it on me.

Awesome. I couldn't even call the locksmith. I'd need to get back in my apartment before morning, even if it meant battering the door down. Roosevelt was still in there, and he'd stage a one-feline riot if his food wasn't a few degrees above room temperature and neatly waiting for him on the table where he could easily knock it all down to the floor and eat it like a barbarian. I'd tried putting it on the floor to begin with once I'd seen his weirdo tendencies, but he liked the power trip of knocking it down. Cats could be assholes.

I hopped up from the couch and tried to gauge my reflection in a framed painting of a rowboat. *A rowboat.* Was that supposed to be symbolic? If it was, I couldn't figure the meaning.

I cringed a little at what I could see of my reflection. I always prided myself on not being *that* girl, the one who has to be perfectly put together for the world to see her, but even I had my limits. My hair was lopsided. My makeup was faded and smeared. I even had a little patch of something that looked like dried drool on my cheek. I grimaced when I thought about how I'd been looking straight into Bob's eyes like this.

I did a quick once-over, as best as I could with my hands and a little bit of spit shine where it was needed. I wasn't going to win any beauty pageants, but at least I wasn't as likely to get mistaken for an escaped mental patient anymore.

The shower water cut off, and I half-jumped my way back to the couch. I rapid-fire cycled through a few positions, trying to find one that made it look like I'd been sitting there, calmly. I sprawled out like I was about to take a nap, decided it was *too* casual. I sat up, crossed my legs, and templed my fingers. *Too serious.* I settled for kicking my feet up on his coffee table and resting my hands on the top of the couch. *Medium casual.*

He stepped out of the bathroom with nothing but a dark gray towel wrapped around his waist. He knew *exactly* what he was doing, and it pissed me off that it was working too well for me to care.

He had all the muscles. Even the obscure little ones that I was never sure if they were ribs or just extra abs. He wasn't so built that he was muscle-bound, but he still looked like he could club you, throw you over his shoulder, and carry you back to his cave where he'd show you that fire wasn't actually man's greatest miracle.

I heard a sound somewhere between a cat purring and growling. It was only a mortified second later that I realized it came from my own throat. I pressed my hand to my chest and cleared my throat. I locked my eyes on him like my life depended on it. "Indigestion," I said quickly. "I ate like three burritos for dinner."

He nodded like I'd just told him something vaguely impressive.

"So... Guess you forgot to bring clean clothes in there with you?" I said through a dry throat, desperate to fill the silence.

"Sure. We can go with that. Or maybe I was just hoping I could figure out if you were a human or a robot."

"I'm definitely a robot. You can look inside if you don't believe me. Just cords, batteries, and plugs. Because I could care less about any of *that*," I gestured to his torso, trying to wear an expression that said it was just so-so while simultaneously diverting all the power in my brain to record a perfect memory of the moment, even if it meant purging non-essential data to make room, like algebra or US history.

"I won't lie," he said. "The thought of getting inside you had crossed my mind."

I felt my eyebrows climbing my forehead. I normally had pretty good control over my face, but right now was too much. All my focus was going into keeping my eyes on his, which wasn't that much help. They were like simmering gray magnets that threatened to pull me in and never let me go.

"Can you put some clothes on before we continue this conversation?" I couldn't take it anymore. I put my hand over my eyes and lowered my head. Let him see my weakness. I didn't care. He was going to see a lot more if I had to keep looking at that, anyway.

"Sure." I heard the towel drop to the ground, and the sound might as well have been a thunderclap.

My brain was on high alert. Naked man. Naked man. Penis flopping in the wind. Buns of steel in plain view. The whole deal. There was a naked man directly in front of me, and all I had to do was peek through my fingers.

I summoned up the willpower to keep my hand right where it was until I heard the door to his bedroom close.

I breathed out a sigh of relief and sank into the couch. *Jesus.* Dying from a sexy-induced heart-attack probably would've been one of the more embarrassing ways for me to go, especially given the reputation I tried to maintain.

"Hey," I said, hoping I was speaking loud enough for him to hear me through the door. "Can I use your phone to call for a locksmith? Mine is still in my apartment."

"What?" he said. The door swung open and he stuck his naked torso out.

"Jesus," I hissed, covering my eyes again. "Stop waving that around, asshole."

He closed the door. "Sorry, thought you said you were choking."

No, you didn't, dickbag. "I said can I use your phone?"

"It's on the coffee table. The password is BOB."

I looked toward the door as if I could read his face through the wood. He was going to just let me open up his phone without supervising me?

I picked it up and tried the password, which, for the record, was probably the dumbest, most insecure password I'd ever heard of. It worked, and I saw the default home screen with what looked like no apps downloaded. He didn't even have any notifications.

I battled my index finger for a few seconds until I managed to overcome the urge to snoop in his photos. I'd always wondered if it was true that men's phone galleries were entirely full of dick pictures, after all.

I pulled up Google and started to search "locksmith" but the browser auto-filled as soon as I typed the "L" with a single suggestion based on his recent searches: "Liam Hightower."

I frowned at the screen for a moment but heard him opening the door from the bedroom and quickly finished typing my search. I punched in my zip code, found a local locksmith, and dialed the number.

"Find one?" he asked.

"Mhm," I said. I hoped I sounded casual, or better—annoyed.

He was wearing a plain white t-shirt now and a pair of sweatpants. It should've looked sloppy or lazy, but of course, it just looked good on him. His hair was still wet and messy, too, which only added to the instinctual desire to throw him down on a bed somewhere and demand at knifepoint that he cuddle the crap out of me. Thankfully, I didn't have a knife.

A few minutes later I found him in the kitchen dumping powder into a shaker cup and then mixing it all up. I handed him his phone. "All yours. The guy will be here in three hours. Said it was the fastest he could do."

"Thanks." He took a long sip of the shake and winced a little.

"Is that a protein shake? Don't those give you really bad gas?" I asked.

He grinned. "I have a strong stomach."

"I saw."

"So you *were* peeking through your fingers?"

I sighed. "No. You practically went Full Monty on me, like six times. I didn't have to peek to see that you are some sort of health freak. Probably wouldn't even eat a jelly bean at gunpoint, would you?"

He pulled open a drawer in the kitchen that was stuffed with what had to be at least six two-pound bags of chocolate covered raisins.

"Seriously?" I asked. "All the sweets in the world and you go for desiccated, chocolate covered grapes?"

"So," he said, ignoring my question. "You can catch some sleep in my bed if you're tired. I can use the couch."

"You think I'm going to go walking into whatever sex dungeon you have set up in your bedroom? No, thanks. I'll sit on the floor, right by the door. That way if you try anything creepy, I can escape faster."

He chuckled. "What qualifies as creepy, exactly? Just trying to make sure I don't scare you off."

"If you have to ask, it's a bad sign."

"Here, I'll make you a deal. You can sit on the floor as long as you let me put a pillow on the ground and give you a blanket."

"Whatever," I said with a shrug.

He grabbed one of the couch cushions and lobbed it to the ground by the door. He came out of his bedroom with what looked like the comforter off his bed.

"Thanks," I said as I sat down on the cushion and pulled the blanket up over my legs. "I guess." The comforter had his smell on it, and I barely resisted the urge to pull it up to my nose and take a huge, embarrassing whiff.

He sat on the floor a few feet away from me and held up his palms at the look I gave him. "Easy there. I'm not trying anything weird. I just thought I'd keep you company. Three hours is a long time to sit and brood."

"Maybe I like brooding."

I expected him to sigh or laugh, but he just looked thoughtful as he let the back of his head rest against the wall. "Me too, sometimes."

"Can't say you struck me as a brooder."

"And I can't say you really know me at all." His tone caught me off guard, but the trace of a smirk in his expression softened the effect.

"Is that an invitation to ask? Not that I care, by the way."

"How about this, you tell me something about you, I tell you something about me. Sound fair?"

"What's your real name?"

"Liam," he said simply. There was no hesitation, but his eyes shifted over to watch me for a reaction.

I only felt vaguely surprised. Liam Hightower, I assumed. So he'd been Googling himself, which shouldn't have surprised me, either. The fact that his name was fake almost seemed like a given. The part I didn't know was why he would be pretending to be someone else. Running from debt? The police? "That makes more sense than Bob. So why are you pretending to be someone else?"

"Nope. It's your turn now. Why are you trying so hard to convince me you're not interested?"

"Maybe because I'm not actually interested?"

"No. You are."

I made an indignant noise, but couldn't quite meet his eyes.

"Tell me I'm wrong, then."

"Even if I was *interested*, that's a pretty vague thing to say. I mean, I'm interested in what happens to our bodies after we die. I'm interested in why clouds are called fog when they're on the ground but not when they're up high. I'm interested in learning to eat a meal without spilling a little bit on my clothes every single time. Or why—"

"Why are you trying to convince me you don't want to sleep with me?"

"Because you think you deserve it?"

He chuckled. "What makes you think that?"

"Look at you." I made a floppy hand gesture toward him. "How many times have you ever had to do more than wink at a girl to get her to strip naked and beg to have sex with you? I feel like I owe it to the world to make it hard for you."

"Well, you've accomplished that. A few times, actually."

Oh, my...

I wasn't a blusher, but my face felt a little hot. I must've been getting a fever. Either way, I wanted to change the subject. "My turn. Why the secrecy? Why are you pretending to be somebody named Bob Smith? And what made you think 'Bob Smith' was a halfway decent alias in the first place?"

"That's two questions, so I'll answer the first. It's my step-sister. She and I had a... disagreement. She thought the best way to get revenge was to plant rumors about me in as many magazines and tabloids as she could. Within a few weeks, I'd come out as gay, declared my intent to get a sex change, described how doctors had printed a list of my STDs, and it was longer than a CVS receipt... I could go on, but you get the idea. She wanted to make sure no woman in the city would come within five feet of me, and it was only a matter of time before the ugly rumors started hurting business."

I raised an eyebrow. "Are these the kind of rumors that have a kernel of truth, or the totally made up kind?"

"Take a wild guess."

"Kernel of truth?"

He glared. "Total fabrications. But it didn't matter. If I publicly denied them, it made them seem more legitimate and brought attention to them. If I ignored them, it looked like I was hiding from the truth. I decided my best option was to hide in plain sight and hope she'd get bored of making my life hell if she couldn't find me."

"Sounds like a really dumb plan."

"What would you suggest?"

"I don't know, give her what she wanted? How bad could it have been?"

"She wanted me to have an affair with her."

"Oh. *Oh.*" I paused while I digested that, then burst out laughing. "I'm sorry," I said. "That's just, well, it's kind of awesome, in a screwed up, deep south kind of way."

He was watching me with a crooked grin. "I'm glad I could get a smile out of you somehow, at least. All it takes is my life to be in shambles."

"I smile sometimes. But I usually only do it around people I like."

"So you're saying you like me? Good. We're making progress."

I gave him a little shrug. "Still deciding. But that was your question. It's my turn again."

He put his thumb to his lip while he locked his eyes on me, and the gesture made my skin feel like it was heating up from the inside-out. His lips were nice. Not quite pouty, but also not stiff and boring. There was such a confidence to his gestures, even the small ones, like the way he would let his head tilt to the side a little as he smiled. I wondered if it was just me, or if anyone with a pulse would find it impossible to tear their eyes away from him.

"Ask away," he said.

"Why are *you* so interested in me?"

"Initially? I thought you were spying on me for my step-sister. But I also thought you had a kind of wounded animal thing going on, too. I've always had a soft spot for broken things."

"Who says I'm broken? You don't have to have a traumatic past to be an asshole."

He laughed. "Then what's your excuse?"

"It wasn't like my parents abused me or anything. They did what most parents do, I guess. They had an idea for what they wanted me to be, and they made it their obsession to see me reach *their* goal." The words practically tumbled out of me. It was a strange sensation, like an overflowing bag suddenly ripping at the seams. Before now, I'd only told my best friend, Emily, about my past, and that had come after years of building trust. Talking to Liam felt natural, though.

He watched me with an intent, focused expression.

"Both my parents were from old money families. My dad's great-grandfather made millions in textiles, and my mom's great-grandfather was a real-estate tycoon in his day. Their grandparents didn't have to work, and they pretty much lived the high life off their inheritances. Houses across the country, exclusive clubs, yachts, all that kind of stuff. By the time the money made it to my mom and dad, they had all the expectations of spoiled rich kids but without the inheritance to match their lifestyle. Their parents had squandered almost everything. The real estate had all been sold in the final years by my grandparents because the money was drying up. They didn't know how to slow down their spending, so they just kept on doing it until they ran dry.

"My parents wanted to have a son so they could groom him to become some kind of business guru. My dad admitted as much a few years ago when he was drunk. When my mom got pregnant with me, they decided to keep trying until they had a son. But a few months after my birth, my mom had to get a hysterectomy. They were devastated, and because they were pessimistic, sexist assholes, they decided they couldn't groom their daughter to be a business mastermind. They wanted to turn me into a turnkey bride—the perfect little easy-open package to be pawned off on the first financially eligible bachelor they could find."

"Damn. He admitted all that to you?"

"Yeah, by the time that conversation happened, you could say I'd already burned a few bridges with them, so our relationship was already rocky anyway. The alcohol helped, too. They thought if I married rich, I'd be their ticket back to the high-money lifestyle."

"So should I be worried that you've shown up in my life? Are you still the turnkey bride just waiting to siphon off my money to your parents?"

I wiggled eyebrows. "Absolutely. You're just a big, fat, sexy piggy bank to me. I'm actually going to text my parents in a few minutes and let them know it's going great so far."

Liam grinned. "You're still a terrible liar."

"Lying wasn't part of my turnkey bride training. But if you need me to balance books on my head while I walk, eat with perfect manners, or do your laundry, I'm very capable. I also know all the English ranks of social status, because that will absolutely be relevant to my daily life. Everyone knows a Duke or a Duchess, right?"

Liam said nothing, but he was watching me with intense interest. It might have been the most intently anyone had ever listened to me talk before, and I felt myself getting that same hot-faced fever feeling again that absolutely wasn't a blush.

"So," I said, clearing my throat. "I did what most kids would do. Once their leash was off, I set out to be exactly what they *didn't* want me to be. Offensive. Sarcastic. Mean. You name it. I'm basically a walking cliche. I thought I was rebelling and I thought I was refusing to be defined by my parents, and in the end I basically let them define me anyway." I laughed a little sadly at that.

"For the record, if you ever feel like not being sarcastic and mean, I won't complain. Then again, you haven't come off as mean to me. Just honest, which I guess is a little ironic since you're saying it's all an act."

I played with my fingers in my lap while my brain churned. "Who knows which one is the real me anymore. Maybe if you play a part long enough, it starts to become real. Or maybe not."

He looked thoughtful. "Well, what makes you happy?"

I shrugged. "I don't know. When stupid people stub their toes or trip and fall? When people are dickholes and karma bites them in the ass?"

He smirked. "I like it. What else makes you happy?"

"When guys I think are jerks turn out to be not so bad."

Liam's eyebrows twitched up. "Who says I'm not so bad? You hardly know anything about me. You didn't even know my real name until a few minutes ago. I could be an absolute prick who's just on his best behavior."

"Well, are you?"

"I like to keep some kind of mystique about me. If you want to find out, I guess you'll have to stick around."

"Hmm." I looked at his sharp features and tried to imagine what kind of man he really was. I'd always believed the average person couldn't hide who they truly were. I'd read once that our resting expressions were gradually shaped by the way we lived our lives. If we spent most of our days scowling, the muscles used to scowl would get stronger and pull our neutral expression toward menacing. Someone who smiled all day would look happier, and so on.

With Liam, I thought I only saw a kind of intense focus in his expression. I could imagine a lifetime of single-minded pursuit of some goal. I could picture him shutting out the world as he tirelessly worked and worked, beyond the capability of a normal person. He was the kind of person the world couldn't touch, I thought—the kind of man you didn't pick because he picked you.

The more I looked at him, the surer I felt that he *had* picked me, and he was choosing to bring me into his life.

"When I look at you," I said. "I just see a guy I would have never imagined taking an interest in a girl like me."

"I don't get distracted easily, and ever since you got your hands on my package, I haven't been able to think about anything else."

"Well," I said, and it felt like I couldn't raise my voice above a husky whisper, as if he'd put some kind of spell over the air itself. I wanted to sound unbothered—even casual—but it felt like a hand softly gripped my throat until I could feel my pulse pounding in my ears. "That's a manipulative choice of words."

"Which part? When I said I can't stop thinking about you, or when I mentioned the way you had your hands all over my package, and I liked it?"

I wasn't sure if the room was shrinking around me, or if he'd scooted closer, but he looked dangerously close to kissing distance.

"Both..."

His fingertip was on the side of my face, tracing a path down from my ear to my jaw that left wonderfully tingly skin and heat everywhere it moved. I closed my eyes and leaned forward, lips pursed. It was automatic. It wasn't something I could've stopped if I wanted to, just like I couldn't have stopped myself from gasping for air if I was drowning.

I felt the first contact of his lips against mine. It wasn't rushed. It was soft and tender. Everything felt like it condensed around us, like my ears closed up and my senses dulled until every last inch of my brain was laser-focused on the kiss—on his lips.

Soft, but firm skin. Warmth. The perfect amount of wetness, and a subtle taste that I could get addicted to. It was bliss, and for those few seconds, I was consumed by him.

So I didn't hear the knocking at first.

I felt the absence of those lips I'd barely begun to experience. I lurched forward, seeking more, but found nothing. When I opened my eyes, he was looking toward the door. "I think your locksmith is here."

Of course he was.

I stood too fast and nearly fell when all the blood rushed to my head. Apparently, it had all been traveling to another part of my body. "Sorry I kissed you," I said. "Not even sure what that was. I don't do the whole spontaneous romantic thing. Probably just still half-asleep."

He stood slowly. "Pretty sure I was the one who kissed you. I don't know if you get credit for just sitting there and taking it."

"Yeah, well, sorry you kissed me, then."

"I'm not."

I gulped. It was a full-on, cartoon-quality, dramatic and embarrassingly loud gulp. "Yeah, well, I should go."

"I'll come by to pick you up tomorrow at seven."

I couldn't seem to find any reason to disagree or change my mind. All I felt was a swirling, excited buzz in my stomach, unlike anything I'd ever experienced. That, and a completely uncharacteristic desire to call Emily up and engage in some serious *girl talk.*

I wasn't stooping to that level. For now, I was going to hold on to as much of my dignity as I could, even when it felt like Liam Hightower was a rushing current of charm, good looks, and swoon-juice trying to uproot me and every grumpy thing I'd ever stood for.

6

LIAM

I woke up groggily with the sense that I wasn't alone. I blinked some of the blurriness from my eyes and could see enough to know that it was still very early. My alarm hadn't gone off, and my bedroom was only lit by the faint blue light from an electronic billboard across the street. For about the dozenth time since I'd been renting this small apartment, I was momentarily shocked to be in a different bed than my own—to see a different view out the windows.

A shadowy figure stood in the doorway.

I bolted upright as a rush of adrenaline blasted away any traces of sleepiness.

"Shame. I was hoping you'd started sleeping nude."

"Celia? What the fuck are you doing in my apartment?"

I flipped the light on and got my first good look at her in a few months. Black hair that was almost always pulled back in a pony-tail. Mischievous brown eyes, and a cruel mouth. As usual, she had so much of her boobs hanging out that it looked like a sneeze would set them free.

Ever since our parents had first married, she had been trying to seduce me. The thought always turned my stomach, but recently, she'd taken it too far, even by her standards.

"I'm here to see you, of course. *Bob*."

"Get out. I can call the cops, or I can just throw you out myself. It's your choice."

She made a sound like a cat's purr. "If you threw me out yourself, you'd have to touch me."

"You're right. I think I have a can of bug spray under the sink. Maybe that would work better."

She curled her lips in a mocking smile. "Liam. I can make all of this stop. All the rumors. The trouble. You just need to give me what I want."

"You're never going to get it."

She laughed. "You still think I want to *fuck* you, don't you? It's not about that. It never was, but I'm not surprised you were always too short-sighted to see it. Every other woman wants to wrap themselves around your fingers, so why wouldn't I?"

I spread my hands out. "I don't know Celia, but maybe you can wrap up the dramatic speech so I can get to the part where I kick you out of my life again."

"I want you to be unhappy, Liam. It's that simple. Maybe some misguided part of me wanted to have you for myself, once, but you lost that opportunity. I spread those rumors because I knew the only thing you cared about was work. But we both know that's quickly becoming untrue, isn't it? You do care about something else, and she lives right... across... the hall."

"Get the fuck out."

Celia laughed again, but this time she actually started walking to the door. "I just wanted to let you know I'm going to make sure I ruin whatever is going on between the two of you, too. And who knows, maybe when I've spoiled your little fling, I'll let you have one night with me as my way of apologizing."

"Out." I pulled the door open and slammed it shut as soon as she was in the hallway.

I pressed my forehead to the wall and closed my eyes while I replayed her threat. I couldn't think of what she could possibly do to screw things up with Lilith and me, but I knew my step-sister well enough to be sure she had a plan.

LILITH SAT DOWN BESIDE ME. WE WERE HAVING BRAZILIAN barbeque, which technically satisfied her request for raw meat. The waiters brought a platter of uncooked steak, chicken, and vegetables to our table along with an assortment of sauces. There was a steaming hot grill in front of us, along with skewers and tongs.

We'd been seated in a relatively private space near the back of the restaurant, which hadn't quite filled up for dinner yet. Guests were seated around stove tops like in a Japanese steakhouse, but it was a more intimate arrangement where everybody cooked their own food and at their own pace. The sound of sizzling food cooking at people's tables and the din of conversation provided its own kind of strange intimacy.

"As requested," I said, gesturing toward the food.

She eyed me. Not for the first time, I was taken back by the sight of her. I'd seen women I found beautiful before, but I'd never felt so addicted to someone. Everything about her seemed to pull me in, from the solitary, freckle above the corner of her mouth to the adorable way she tried to seem so hard. I knew it wasn't *all* an act, but it felt like I could see straight through the smoke and mirrors with her. I saw the sweet girl on the inside, the one she was afraid to show anybody. I saw the insecurity that made her put up walls and push people away. They didn't scare me, and they never would.

"You did know I was only messing with you about the raw meat thing, right?" Lilith asked.

"I might have had a bit of doubt, if I'm honest."

She actually smiled at that. The rarity of her smiles made

them feel precious, and I see how hooked I could become on chasing the next one. Lilith's pale skin looked creamy and soft against the fabric of her dress. It was a dark purple with an exposed back but a high neckline. Her black hair was tied up over her head in a simple but attractive style. Then again, I think I might've already reached the dangerous point where just about anything on her would suit my tastes.

I marveled at how quickly it was happening. The change she was making spread through me. Where I'd felt cold and detached only a few days ago, I already could sense something stirring. It wasn't that I hadn't had an interest in dating, not entirely anyway. I'd just found less and less time to spend pursuing relationships, until I eventually all-but stopped. Chasing after Lilith didn't feel like time I had to carve out of my workday. It felt more like my workday now needed to fit itself around whatever schedule my hunt for Lilith demanded.

"You know," I said. I was wrapping a piece of beef in some lettuce like I'd seen a colleague do a few years back—it had been my first experience with Brazilian barbecue. I wasn't sure if it was proper technique, but it had tasted good. "I haven't done this in a long time."

"Date?" She asked. Her eyes followed my movements. She mimicked me, setting the little package of meat down on the table and dousing it with sauce to steam.

"Yeah. I think it has been three years, maybe more. I just fell out of the habit, I guess."

"I don't think dating is supposed to seem like an obligation. It's not flossing or mowing the lawn. You're supposed to want to do it."

"What about you, then?" I absentmindedly tossed a few vegetables on the grill to join the meat. Lilith mirrored my movements again.

"I just so happened to have not wanted to do it, for a pretty long time."

"How long, exactly?"

"I don't know. Six or seven?"

"Months?"

"Years..."

I laughed. "And you were giving *me* a hard time?"

She shrugged. "I don't pretend to be a normally functioning person like you."

"Hey, now. I never claimed to be normally functioning. Didn't I tell you my step-sister is trying to ruin my life because I wouldn't have an affair with her?"

Her lips twitched up at the corners. "That rings a bell."

My own smile faded when I thought of Celia and the conversation I'd had with her earlier that morning. "She's just the beginning, and let's leave it at that because I don't want to spoil your appetite with the full story."

Lilith met my eyes, and there was something in her expression that I couldn't quite decide what to make of. It was either frightening, or sexy, or maybe both. "Do you want me to take care of this step-sister of yours? I can tell her I'm about to pop out her perfect step-brother's baby, so she might as well call it quits. Or, you know, I could just stab her in her sleep."

"So you think I'm perfect, do you?"

She rolled her eyes, but there was a glimmer of humor in her features. "*That* was your takeaway?"

I shook my head and focused off into the distance. "You don't want to make Celia think there's anything serious between us. It'd only egg her on more."

"So? Is she ever going to stop if you don't confront her?"

"I can't imagine a scenario where she really 'stops.' I can picture her getting bored for a while, but I don't think it'll ever end. Not entirely."

"Then we egg the bitch on."

I laughed at the intensity in her voice. "You know, a few hundred years ago, I think you would have made a really good spy or assassin. Actually, not a spy. Your little espionage operation at the coffee shop was a pretty big bust, but I can absolutely see you stabbing someone."

She flashed that rare smile of hers, and I drank in every second of it.

"One: I wasn't spying on you, so you can stop flattering yourself. I just happened to be carrying around my bird watching gear, which could be mistaken for spy gear. You were the one who went all psycho and chased me into the subway. Two: I'm not sure if the stabbing thing was meant as a compliment, but I'm taking it as one."

I pointed to our food sizzling on the table. "We should turn these. Pull the meat out of the lettuce and let it sit on the grill for just a minute or two so it sears now."

She nodded and followed my movements, then stirred up her vegetables along with me. They had already started to blacken along the edges.

"This place is kind of cool," she said. "I feel like a cavewoman."

"You handle your utensils like one," I noted.

She glared at me. "Want to find out if I can handle the knife better than these goofy tongs?"

"It's not a knife I want to see you handle."

She looked confused for a few seconds, then her eyes widened slightly and she stared back toward the food. "Can I say something honest? And I want you to promise you're not going to think I'm digging for some lame compliment, okay?"

"Yeah," I said. My stomach lurched a little at her question. Qualifiers like that usually meant somebody was about to tell you they didn't think it was going to work out after all, or that they have a terminal illness, or that you've had a giant piece of food in your teeth all night. "Go ahead."

"I can't stop feeling like all of this is a practical joke. You're not the type of guy who asks me on dates, and you're definitely not the type of guy who has ever seemed interested in sleeping with me. Can you just promise me this isn't a joke?"

"What? Why would you even think I'd mess around about something like that?"

She shrugged, and all her hard edges seemed to melt away. For a few seconds, I thought I saw what she hid so well behind the sarcasm and the dark humor. She didn't push people away because she was mean or cruel, she pushed them away because she was afraid of getting hurt, of showing them the real Lilith and getting mocked or rejected. "I guess experience has taught me to be skeptical when people are nice?"

I wanted to ask her what happened, but it didn't feel like the right time. She didn't need to dig up her old ghosts right now, she just needed to feel secure. She needed me to convince her that she could feel safe when she was with me—that I'd never take any part of her for granted.

I slid my hand into hers under the table and gripped it as I met her eyes. "How about this. I'll give you a key to my apartment. If I ever give you a reason to think I have tried to trick you somehow, you can come in at night and do the whole stabbing thing you're so into."

She bit back a crooked smile. "I don't *actually* like stabbing things. It's just one of those things I say because it freaks people out."

"Well it works," I laughed. "I'm serious, though. I'd never try to trick you. I asked you on a date because I felt a connection. I wanted to get to know you because I think you're interesting. And I wanted to sleep with you because, well, look at you."

"You weren't supposed to compliment me. Now I feel like I was fishing for that."

"You're burning."

"Huh? Is that how the cool guys are saying 'hot' now? Because it's kind of lame."

"No," I grinned. "Your food."

She peeled her food from the grill, which had started to skirt the line between charred and burnt. "Yours isn't looking so great, either."

"Totally intentional. It's blackened. That's all."

"I think it's more like carbonized."

I cut off a slice of the meat and popped it in my mouth. I chewed into the thick shell of burnt matter and my mouth was blasted with an ashy, bitter taste. I felt my eyes watering as I forced myself to swallow. "No way. Totally delicious." I coughed into my hand and then shrugged. "Or not."

I knew it was a successful date, at least on some level, because the burnt food didn't spoil our moods. We ate around the worst parts, talked, and I even managed to squeeze another laugh or two out of Lilith before the bill was paid.

We shared a cab back to our apartments. It had just been a little chilly when we were leaving for the restaurant, but a more biting cold had quickly settled in as the night drew on.

We stood on the sidewalk outside our building while a few people came and went around us. Lilith was clutching her arms around herself, and I pulled her in toward my chest without thinking. She was stiff at first, but then she relaxed, resting her head against my chest. I slid my hands up her back and squeezed her into me. It felt good to hold her. *Damn good.*

I looked up into the darkness between the skyscrapers above us and saw the first specks of snow start swirling down. I closed my eyes, trying hard to memorize the moment. It shouldn't have been anything remarkable. One date. One long hug. She should have just been another girl that would end up drifting out of my life.

I didn't buy it, though. I'd never wanted to hold on to someone this badly. This desperately. Was it only because Celia was trying so hard to ruin things for me? Maybe my fixation on Lilith was nothing but a competitive urge to prove I could keep a relationship alive despite Celia's best efforts.

Maybe. But I doubted it. I didn't think I could fool myself this well. What I felt seemed real.

I felt my fingers press a little harder against her back, and she let out a soft, contented sigh.

"You're so warm. Like a werewolf from Twilight. Are you really a werewolf, *Bob Smith*?"

I smirked. "There won't be a full moon for another few weeks. If you want to find out, I guess you're going to just have to stick around."

"Damn. I was hoping this was going to just be a one-night stand." She stiffened again, and I could almost picture the surprise on her face.

Hadn't planned to admit you were thinking about sleeping with me, had you?

"So you're saying sex *is* on the table?" I asked.

"I usually prefer it on a bed."

I slid my hand into her purse and found the metallic ring of her keychain. I slid it out and dangled it in front of her eyes. I shoved them in my pocket and gave her a meaningful look. "I think you forgot your keys in your apartment again. Looks like you'll need to hang out in my place for a couple hours while we wait for a locksmith."

She raised an eyebrow. "What do you take me for, some kind of harlot who will jump at any excuse to hook up with you?"

We didn't make it past the entryway of his apartment before he had me pinned to the wall. His mouth was hot and hungry against mine. I felt like I'd been swept up in the current of somebody else's life. I'd had sex before. *Sort of.* If a fumbling, awkward encounter in my high school years counted. It hadn't felt like a compulsion, not like this, like something deep inside my chest clawing to get out.

I had my doubts about Liam. I'd met the man under a false name, for starters, but I couldn't deny the connection I felt on a basic level. We clicked. It was as simple as that. After tonight, who knew where it would go, but right now, I didn't want to fight my instincts. I wanted to put on a blindfold, handcuff myself, and let my instincts take over.

His hands were so strong against me. They slid up my leg, forcing my dress up with them into a bunched up mess of fabric.

Kissing him was intoxicating. My brain didn't wander. Every ounce of my focus was on the moment. On us. It was like being submerged in warm, glittering water, at least if that water knew how to French kiss and had a fondness for squeezing asses.

"Am I supposed to ask if we should be doing this?" I breathed between kisses. "That's the dainty thing to say at a time like this, right?"

"What do you mean?" He pulled his face back enough to meet my eyes. His fingertips played against the skin of my face with a frightening tenderness.

I'd grown up deeply entrenched in a school of tough love, and my parents had never been ones for hugging, kissing, and cuddling. The way Liam was touching me triggered a deep-seated need. I wanted to melt into his hands

"I feel like I'm supposed to act like I have my doubts right now," I said. "You know, so you don't think I'm too eager to sleep with you. Preserve the pure virgin thing and all that."

He smirked. "I don't care if you're a pure virgin. I want you to want this as much as I do. Fuck all the unwritten rules. I just want you to myself right now. All of you."

I bit my lip. "Then take me to your bed, because if I have to wait any longer, I think I'm going to explode."

He gripped the back of my thighs and hoisted me up so I was clinging to him like an over-sized child with my hands threaded behind his neck. I let him carry me through his apartment and to his bed, where he surprised me by tossing me down on the bed. I almost giggled as I landed. *Giggled.* I didn't care how much I was enjoying myself, if there was one thing I wasn't going to do, it was *giggle.*

I settled for a suppressed smile as I looked up at him. He pulled his shirt off, and this time, I didn't look away. I let my eyes move molasses-slow across every last rippling muscle of his torso, the hard lines and pleasant planes that refused to release my eyes. There was a natural path as I looked down the line of his body, like a well-planned painting that has one goal: to draw the eye down, and down, and *down.*

I was mesmerized as his hands went to his belt and flicked the latch free. The weight of the buckle dangling dragged the waistband of his pants down just enough to let me see the elastic of his underwear. A gray waistband and black, tight-fitting boxers.

In that moment, I questioned every lie I'd ever told myself about the ability of a dildo to replace a man, no matter how high quality the device may be. I never got to watch my dildo undress. I could never smell the manliness radiating off of a dildo, like some pheremonal cocktail that lit rocket-fuel under my ovaries and propelled them straight into my brain. *Babies. Babies. Babies.* I'd never seriously considered having kids, but when I looked up at Liam towering over me, I could imagine a dark-haired little sarcastic child in my life, and I could imagine how hot it would be to feel Liam finding his release inside me.

I pumped the mental brakes, though. Hot was one thing. Practical was another. At least some part of my head was still functioning in the real world, even while ninety percent of my brain was drooling over him. I wanted to make it in business, maybe even own my own company one day. The last thing I needed to mix into the equation was a kid.

His pants dropped and my jaw followed.

Beautiful bulge.

Our kissing had clearly done the job of getting him ready to go, and if the pulsing heat I felt between my own legs was any indication, I was just as ready.

"This only works if we both take off our clothes," he said.

"Oh, really? So you're telling me what they taught about reproduction in Sunday school was a lie?"

He leaned over me and slid the straps of my dress down over my shoulders. "I think you ever attending Sunday school is a lie, because they don't teach you about reproduction there."

"Who says I'm not religious?"

His eyes didn't move away from where he was slowly stripping away my dress, almost ritualistically. He was clearly savoring every inch of skin he unwrapped, as if I was a life-sized Christmas present. "Are you?"

"Maybe. But I don't reveal my secrets so easily."

"Secrets, huh?" he bent down and pressed his mouth to my breasts, just above my bra.

I gasped, arching my back toward him involuntarily. An unstoppable fire was growing inside me, and I knew the only thing that could quench it was him. I needed him. On top of me. Surrounding me. *Inside me.*

"Well," he said as he lifted his head again and kissed me once on the mouth. "Whether you're religious or not, I think you're going to take the Lord's name in vain a few times before I'm done with you."

I bit back a smile. "Is that a challenge?"

"It can be."

"Just watch, then."

"Don't worry. I wasn't planning on taking my eyes off you any time soon."

He pulled away the last of my dress and sat back on his knees, devouring me with his eyes again. Nobody had ever looked at me the way he was. It wasn't blind lust or casual attraction. When he looked at me, he seemed *moved*. I could imagine the gears in that beautiful head of his churning, thoughts racing as his mind tried to grasp some concept that it couldn't quite sink its teeth into. But what was it? What was he trying to figure out?

He sat me up and reached to unhook my bra. I felt him tug at the clasp for a few seconds before he gave me an apologetic look. "I think it's stuck."

"This one does that. Let me just—"

"No," he said. "I got this." He yanked his hands apart and I heard the stomach-churning sound of my fifty-dollar bra snapping open against its will.

Despite the fact that my breasts were breaking free in front of a man for the first time in years, all I could think was that he'd just broken my favorite bra—the one that made my boobs look like perfectly symmetrical, perky little grapefruits. Well, apples, maybe. Or something just a little smaller, but the point was it made them look good, and the big brute wanted to play caveman and tear the thing off me.

"Do you know how hard it is to find a good bra?"

"I'll buy you another one." He leaned in to kiss me again, but I put my finger to his lips.

"I got that at a store that went out of business. Unless you have a time machine, I don't think you will."

"I'll learn to sew and put it back together for you."

I glared, but had to hold back a smile as an idea occurred to me. "You *are* going to make it up to me, but it's not going to be with a sewing kit. I want you to spell the alphabet for me."

"Spell... You realize the alphabet isn't 'spelled,' right? It's all just individual letters, and what does—"

I pointed down to my panties, which embarrassingly already had developed a wet spot from all the kissing and undressing that had gone on.

He looked confused. "Spell the... Oh. You mean on your? *Oh...*"

I don't know why I thought it would sound like a punishment to him, because it looked like I'd just offered him a treat instead. He hooked his fingers in my panties and slid them off before tossing them to the floor.

And just like that, I was naked as the day I was born, while he still had his boxers on. I'd fix that, but it could wait.

I held my hand over myself as I met his eyes. I may have been talking a confident game, especially when I'd made my last little order, but the truth was I felt like curling up and hiding on the inside. My lone sexual experience had been prom night in high school. I'd only been eighteen a couple months, and I'd fallen for the classic "just the tip" tactic. As it turned out, neither of us understood that lubrication was essential, natural or otherwise, and we'd spent ten minutes of futility while he prodded at me and I eventually had to call the entire thing off.

Depending on how you wanted to classify things, that probably made me a virgin, if the silicone penises didn't count, that was.

I couldn't look away as he brought his head down between my legs. I had an amazing view of his broad, muscular back from where I laid against the pillows. His hands were firm around my thighs and his eyes met mine for a taunting second that seemed to say, *you're about to get more than you bargained for.*

He put his mouth over me and started doing *exactly what I had demanded.*

First, his tongue traced out the shape of an "A", then a "B", and by the time we made it to "M," I was in trouble. All my ideas that I was in control evaporated. He was the master here. With nothing but the tip of his tongue, he had me at his complete mercy. *And I liked it.*

I spent so much effort trying to make sure I was never beneath anyone. I'd tried so hard to shake off my parent's attempts to turn me into the perfect little pre-packaged bride. I didn't want to be the girly girl who liked to wear pink and wanted to let a guy pamper her. But somewhere along the line, I think I tried so hard to get away from the stereotype that I cornered myself into another one.

For once, it felt amazing to let go of it all and just be free of expectations and self-doubt. What he was doing felt good, and I wanted him to do it. It was that simple.

"God, Liam," I moaned. "Can you just spell out 'mmm'?"

"Got it," he said, but the bastard knew what he was doing when he barely moved away from me as he spoke. His lips brushed all the right places and made me shake with pleasure. "And I already got you to take the Lord's name in vain. Did they cover that in Sunday school?"

"I don't care anymore, as long as you keep doing what you're doing."

He chuckled, and even the rumble of his laugh sent shock-waves of pleasure through me.

The sound of his phone buzzing with a text message on the nightstand drew Liam's attention. He flicked his eyes toward it, then did a double take. Despite the fact that I was butt-ass naked with my legs spread around his head, the man had the nerve to actually reach across me for his phone.

"Seriously?" I asked.

"I'm sorry, I just need to be sure..." His face went pale as soon as he read whatever the text message said. He glanced toward the nearest window. I could see his jaw muscles flexing and relaxing again and again like he was trying to chew through something impossibly tough.

"Did you get bored, or something? *Liam?*" I sat up, snapping my fingers in front of his face. "Forget it," I said. All the pleasant emotions and feelings that had been throbbing within me trans-formed in an instant. The old, familiar cynicism and darkness crept back in. I moved away from him and his half-hearted attempts to stop me, gathered my clothes, and dressed. I wanted to be away from this moment as fast as I could, from the reality that I'd stripped away all my defenses so easily for him, and for what? A memory I probably wouldn't be able to look back on without thick, ugly waves of shame?

"It's a family thing," he muttered. "It wasn't you, at all. You—"

"Save it. You're good looking and charming, so you got one stupid act out of me. *One.* That's more than most people get. I hope you enjoyed it, because it's not happening again."

I fast-walked out of his apartment with as much dignity as I could manage. As soon as the door closed behind me, I realized with a sinking stomach that I'd forgotten my purse, along with my keys, inside his place. I pulled the door open to find him standing in the doorway, still bare-chested.

He didn't wear any of the cocky confidence from before on his face. There was only regret there as he reached out to hand me my purse and keys. "Can I explain tomorrow at least? Just have lunch with me."

I took the purse and keys from him without a word and left. I could still feel the heat and wetness of his mouth between my legs, and I could hardly believe how quickly it had all turned from amazing to horrible. I should've figured. The more I looked back on my life, the more I saw how everything I'd been through played out more or less the same. It started full of promise, and as soon as I let my walls down and got excited, it turned to crap. My best friend had left for another country. Stupid "Bob Smith" had left me with a thousand questions about what kind of text would make him stop in the middle of eating me out and lose all interest. Even my parents, years ago, had eventually written me off as a lost cause.

At least I had my cat. If there was one thing to appreciate about Roosevelt, it was that he'd never bothered trying to make me believe our relationship was going to be special. He was completely open. I was just the human he tolerated, so long as I kept him fed and occasionally let him play with an empty box. There were no unknowns in the cat and human relations department. He used me for food or just for the enjoyment of waking me up several times a night while he aggressively groomed himself, but I knew the deal.

I'd been cock blind, as the saying went. I had a perfectly acceptable situation going for myself. An unfulfilling job that barely gave me time to work towards my real dreams, a lack of fulfilling personal relationships, and a growing sense of disillusionment with the world and my future. Life was fine, and then I made the same mistake women have been making for centuries. I thought I needed the meatbag attached to the penis. Technology gave me the means to separate the penis from the man, and somehow, someway, I'd let my idiot neighbor convince me that technology had led me down the wrong path.

Never again. *Probably*, at least. Unless he really nailed the apology. Or if he had a really, *really* good excuse. I'd maybe even consider bribery acceptable, if it was edible. I hated admitting it, but I had a feeling once the embarrassment of what just happened wasn't as fresh, I'd start wondering what could have been between us.

I flopped down on my bed, face-first and sighed into the pillow.

Roosevelt jumped up and walked a smug little circle on my back, and then began cleaning his butthole like his life depended on it. I groaned in disgust and did an alligator death-roll to get him off. He flopped to the floor with a thump and an annoyed little meow.

"No boys in my bed tonight," I said. "Not even you, Roosevelt." Unsurprisingly, he didn't listen.

8

LIAM

I picked up my car from a parking garage a few blocks away from my apartment. I hadn't used the car since I planned the entire incognito operation, and, as it turned out, I could've saved myself a whole lot of hassle by skipping the stunt in the first place. My step-sister had never really been thrown off my scent, it seemed. If anything, it had actually convinced her she really was getting to me and it just egged her on.

I probably should've turned in my keys to the apartment as soon as she visited me in my room, but the truth was I'd liked the idea of living across from Lilith more than the thought of my million-dollar apartment in the heart of downtown. I'd even grown to enjoy the separation, however artificial, from my old life. I was pretending to be someone else, and part of that act had me sidelining work more than I had in years. The old me might not have even had his head out of his ass long enough to notice Lilith. Then again, the old me lived in an obnoxiously expensive penthouse above an obnoxiously luxurious hotel downtown. There were no girls like Lilith in my old life.

Everybody in my old life was consumed by money. It was strange to think how exciting that old life had seemed once. Business was taking off, and in a blur of months, it felt like the price tags fell off the world. Anything could be mine if I just reached for it and took it. It was a reward that seemed to justify my obsession with work, and I let it be my excuse to bury myself in work for far longer than I should have. Becoming "Bob Smith" had given me a fresh perspective.

And it had given me Lilith. At least until last night, it had.

Even thinking of Lilith stung. I'd replayed the last few hours so many times I had lost count. I'd thought of at least a hundred ways I could've handled it better—ways I could've reacted that wouldn't have sent Lilith storming out of my apartment, and maybe my life. But the moment I saw the text from Celia, my blood had boiled.

The text was burned into my brain. It had said, "Wow. This spy camera is super high definition. Is that the alphabet you're spelling between her legs?"

She must have hidden the camera on the morning she came into my apartment, and she must have been watching every second of what was happening between Lilith and I. Violated didn't even begin to describe how I felt. I couldn't believe I hadn't even thought to do a look around my apartment to see if she'd done anything after *breaking in.*

I was pissed, and I was parked outside Celia's house. More accurately, it was her senator husband's house outside the city. It was just after three in the morning, but I didn't let that stop me. I'd find a way to make things right with Lilith soon, but before I could do that, I had to put a stop to this childish, disgusting bullshit Celia was pulling.

It was a big house, and not the tasteful kind of big. It was more like the "look how superior I am to you" kind of way. Roman-style pillars and tall archways decorated the exterior, and I knew from my previous visits that the interior was even more ostentatious. I think there was even a nude sculpture and cherubs inside, as if I needed any more reason to hate my step-sister and her husband.

I knocked hard on the door. Well, it was somewhere between a knock and hoping I accidentally slammed my fist through the wood. I waited two seconds and hammered on the door again.

"Open the goddamn door," I shouted. "Open the—"

The door swung open to reveal Celia's husband, Walter Normandy. Walter was about thirty years older than Celia and I with a proud, bowling-ball belly and a gray walrus mustache. The hair on top of his head had long since retired, which completed the walrus look. He was wearing a wife-beater that did a poor job of hiding the wooly mane of body hair that sprouted out of his torso in thick tufts, and the look on his face said I'd clearly woken him up.

"You?" he growled.

"Yeah, me, asshole. Where is your wife?"

Walter puffed up his chest and tried to look down his nose at me, which didn't work very well considering he was at least a foot shorter than I was.

"I'll give you a minute to get back in your car and get the fuck off my property."

Celia emerged from behind him and put a calming hand on his shoulder. She stood a few inches taller than him, and when she looked down at her stooped husband, I saw her lips curl. "It's quite alright. Why don't you get back to bed? You've got a big day tomorrow, and I want my big, fuzzy bear to be well-rested." Her tone was patronizing, like she was talking to a small child, but if Walter noticed, he gave no sign of it.

He looked up at her, and all the anger he'd shown me a moment ago melted away to absolute adoration. He puckered his lips out for a kiss. Celia bent down and pecked her lips against his without taking her eyes from me.

Walter hobbled back into the house and Celia stepped

outside, closing the door. With a practiced, smooth motion, she wiped her lips with the back of her hand, then wiped the back of her hand on her nightgown. "I presume you're here to make some kind of macho threats because of the text I sent?" She leaned close to my face and breathed in through her nose. "I think I can still smell her pussy on you. You really didn't waste any time, did—"

"It's done." My voice was nearly a growl. "Whatever this shit is. Whatever you think is going to come of it. It's done. If I even *think* you're still fucking around with my life, I'll do everything in my power to get you thrown in jail or sued for everything your worth. I'll ruin you. I swear it."

She rolled her eyes. "Liam," she cooed. "You're so sexy when you're mad." She reached to touch my cheek, but I flinched back from her touch. "But you're really just a big, dumb, gorgeous hunk of meat. Unless you were planning some sort of... *physical* incident, you're powerless. I've covered every base. Every little thread you probably think you could pull to unravel me is only a dead end. There's nothing you can do, Liam. Except give in, of course, but I know you're stubborn, so I'm prepared to wait as long as it takes."

"Stay. Away." I was too mad to say more, to articulate my thoughts, or to explain how wrong she was. It didn't matter, anyway. I almost wanted her to try again, to give me an excuse. Thinking I was incapable would be the worst mistake she could make. Maybe she'd assumed I had been trying to get back at her this whole time, but I'd only been weathering the storm. I didn't want to turn this ridiculous fixation of hers into a full-blown war, but now? Now she'd gotten her filthy hands between Lilith and me, and I was ready to do whatever it took to shut her down.

She tutted. "Is that all? No big speech or grand threats? Just 'stay away?'" she asked, forcing her voice down deep to mimic mine. "Oh, by the way. Next time, take your boxers off before you go down on her. I was so disappointed that you left them on."

"What happened to the things you said yesterday morning? This isn't about sex? Just revenge?" I shook my head in disgust.

She flicked her eyebrows up and tilted her heads. "*Whoops.* Did I fib? You can cuff me, if that will make you feel better." Celia held out her wrists and pouted her lips.

"How long did you say the jail time is for murder?" I asked Price.

"Celia is a bitch," he said, "but I don't think I can help you plan her murder. That's probably a step too far. Pretty sure there's some special clause in the bible for people who kill their siblings."

We were in my office downtown. It was my first time back at work in what felt like weeks. I still hadn't completely shed my half-assed double life as "Bob Smith," mainly because I wasn't even close to giving up on Lilith, and I wasn't exactly itching to reclaim my old life just yet. Plus, I needed to keep an eye out in case she got it in her head to invite some other guy over to make me jealous. It would absolutely work, and I wasn't above making an ass of myself to step in to keep something like that from happening.

"You mean hiding a camera in my apartment and pointing it at my bed wasn't a step too far?"

Price tilted his head and considered. "There's peeping, and then there's murder. In the eyes of the law, I'm pretty sure one of those is more frowned upon."

"What about humane murder?" I asked. "Would you still be opposed if—"

"Yes. If it's with a bazooka or a spoon, I'm not going to approve the murder of my sister. Sorry."

I sighed. "I'd be letting her off too easy, anyway. She needs to have a long time to regret pissing me off. Years and years of disappointment. I want her to marinate in depression until you can smell it coming off her as soon as she walks in a room."

Price raised his eyebrows at me and grinned a little. "She's got you pretty pissed, huh?"

I leaned back in my chair and stared out the window. "A little. Yeah."

"Is it because of the camera, or is it because her stunt made you fuck things up with the neighbor girl?"

"Can't it be both?"

"I'm just saying. You're normally a pretty easy-going guy, Liam. Hell, when she started putting you through this shit, you decided to play nice and disappear until she got bored. God knows you could've struck back a month ago when this began. So why all the sudden anger if it's not because of the girl?"

"So it's because of the girl, then. What difference does it make? I'm done dealing with Celia's bullshit. I meant what I said to her, too. If she tries to get involved one more time, even in the smallest way, I'm not holding anything back."

"What do you mean, like you'll burn her house down?"

"I was exaggerating with the murder stuff, Price. I'm not insane. I don't want to kill her, I just want her to wake up every day and think to herself, 'my life is ruined. I royally fucked up when I decided to cross Liam Hightower. I'm a mistake, and the world would be a better place without me.'"

"Wow, yeah. You're not insane at all."

9

LILITH

I left extra early for work, which was absolutely not my style. I had a feeling Liam would come knocking on my door in the morning and try to smooth-talk me into forgiving him. When it came to him, I couldn't trust myself. So, like an addict, I didn't even give myself the opportunity to fall for the trap.

I set my alarm for five in the morning, got ready as quickly as I could, and was out of the apartment by six.

Thankfully, it was an odd day of work, and I was able to keep Liam off my mind for most of the morning. William's twin brother, Bruce, and William's grandmother-in-law had a secret meeting with me to talk about plans for William's surprise birthday party.

I sat across from Bruce in his neat and tidy corner office while William's grandmother-in-law, A.K.A "Grammy" paced around and continually touched everything, turned it, or moved it just a few centimeters to one side. Every time she fidgeted with something in Bruce's office, I could see the twinkle of mischief in her eyes. She knew Bruce was a neat-freak bordering on O.C.D., and more than anyone I'd ever met, Grammy was a button-pusher.

Bruce had to pause our little meeting to take a call, but he was getting visibly worked up over Grammy's meddling.

"How's your dark little life treating you?" Grammy asked me. She ran her fingertips over the blinds behind Bruce's desk, tilting a few random sections out of alignment with the others.

"Just waiting for the next disappointing turn of events. What about you, planning on dying any time soon?"

She barked a laugh. "The moment you plan to die is the moment you stop living."

"Nice. Did you read that on a Hallmark card?"

"Fortune cookie."

"Where's Hailey, anyway?" I asked. "Isn't she the one who should have to plan the birthday party for that idiot?"

"I didn't invite her because she'd try to talk us out of doing anything cool. You feel me, fam?"

"Ugh," I said, but I almost couldn't stop myself from grinning. "It's so gross when you try to talk 'hip.' Can you please not do that? It's such a cliché old person thing. You realize that, right? You didn't invent trying to make young people uncomfortable by using their words."

"You're too young to know what I did or didn't invent, squirt. And it's only cliché if I'm not aware, which I am, which makes it *meta*. And no, I'm not going to explain what that means to you."

I sighed. "Whether it's 'meta' or not, it's gross. You should just use old people words like whippersnapper and hooligan instead of talking like a seven-year-old."

"Is it also gross if I tell you that I just got some action last night and I'm still feeling sore? Can't tell if it's because he did a good job or if it's because I'm in my seventies, but damn my hammies are tight today."

"Yes. That's also gross."

She shrugged as she lifted up a paperweight from Bruce's desk. I thought his eyes might bulge out of their sockets when she tossed it casually from one hand to another and then set it back down, just a few inches from where she'd picked it up. "There's a reason all the pipes keep running late into old age."

"Whether your 'pipes' are running or not is definitely in the category of things I don't need to know."

Grammy laughed. "Then I wouldn't get to see the horrified look on your face. What fun would that be?"

"I'm not horrified. It's just gross to picture."

"What if I told you we did butt stuff, mouth stuff, *and* pussy stuff, and it all happened in an order that would surprise you."

I raised my eyebrows and stared toward Bruce, who had ended his call and was looking back at me with the same horrified expression. "Then yes," I said quietly. "That would horrify me."

She cackled again. "Finally off the phone, boss man? It's about time. Some of us don't have much longer on this Earth, you know."

"I'm sure you'll live for many, *many* more years to come," Bruce said. "I think you're too stubborn to die."

"Good. At least you're not a complete idiot, like your brother."

"William is eccentric," Bruce said. "He's not an idiot, unfortunately. If he was an idiot, I could just write him a check every month and keep him out of my life and our business. Unfortunately, I actually need what he brings to Galleon, so we're all forced to endure him."

"Agree to disagree," I said.

Bruce grinned. "Unlike some of you, I actually have work to do. So could we skip to the part where we plan this birthday party?"

"Male strippers," Grammy said. "That's it. I don't need your input or your opinions. It's happening. I just need you for your money," she said, pointing to Bruce. "And I need you to work with his wifey to think up a good cover story to get him to show up at the right time and without a clue. Bonus points if you can think of a cover story that gets him to show up wearing something stupid. I'll handle the costumes for the strippers and everything else."

I nodded in approval. "I like it."

Bruce shook his head. "If I agree to this, does it mean you'll leave my office and stop touching my things?"

I WAS EXTRA TIRED BY THE TIME I GOT OFF WORK. I'D WOKEN UP almost two hours before my usual time that morning. I'd also stayed up a few hours later than normal last night because of the combination of remembering how amazing it had felt to have Liam between my legs and the confusion of trying to figure out what the hell had made him flip a switch so quickly.

I paused outside the door to my apartment complex and tried to peek in the window. I didn't want to run into him. Liam didn't have my phone number, at least, so if I could manage to come and go without him seeing me, I could avoid him.

"I think it's clear," a voice said from behind me.

I jumped away from the sound. On the streets of New York City, unexpected voices over your shoulder raised all kinds of red flags. When I turned around to face him, I was ready to gouge eyeballs with my pinky fingers if I had to. I relaxed, but only a little, when I saw it was Liam.

"What were you doing, just creeping around until I got here?" I asked.

Liam gave a little tilt of his head to acknowledge the accusation. "Kind of. I did take a few breaks. Got a hotdog. Talked to a homeless guy about taxes. Fed some bread to a pigeon. But yeah, pretty much just waited here till you showed up."

He was wearing a suit and tie that looked expensive. I didn't know enough about clothes to say for sure, but I had a suspicion his clothes meant he had cast away the middle-class Bob Smith persona, at least as far as his wardrobe was concerned. I knew enough to know he was probably very wealthy, but seeing him dressed up really hammered the point home.

I had been right, after all. Even when I'd seen him dressing down, I could practically smell the fancy yacht-dweller scent radiating off him.

"I've got important things to do. There's a marathon of *Boy Meets World* starting in ten minutes, so..."

"Wow, yeah," he said. "That sounds pretty important. I could go grab a pizza and we could watch it together."

I held up a finger in his face and shook my head. "No. You don't get to just schmooze your way back into my good graces. I made a rare exception for you. I was *nice* to you, and if—"

"Let me explain."

I shook my head and reached for the door, but he put his hand on top of mine and stopped me.

"Lilith. I'm not letting that dumb thing that happens in shows and movies happen here. I can seriously explain what happened. Just hear me out."

I crossed my arms. "What dumb thing?"

He shrugged. "You know. Where there's a simple explanation, but instead of just spitting it out, the character keeps saying things like, 'wait, if you just let me explain,' and 'don't go! I can explain.' Except they repeat ten versions of that instead of just spitting out the three words that would fix everything. So half the movie goes by with a misunderstanding that could be fixed if the characters just talked for five seconds."

"So you're telling me you have three magic words that can fix everything?"

Liam looked up, and I could tell he was trying to arrange whatever he was going to try to say into three words. "There wassah camera."

"Wassah?" I asked.

"Four words would have been better. But yes. There was a camera."

"Wait," I said. His words finally sank in. "You were filming us? I'm waiting for the part where this magically fixes anything, except making sure I don't feel any guilt when I murder you in your sleep."

"Remember the step-sister I told you about? She broke into my apartment yesterday morning and gave some ridiculous, evil villain speech. I thought it was just her being dramatic, but she must have hidden the cameras before she woke me up."

"Cameras? Plural? Are you saying there's a video of me on the internet somewhere by now?"

"No. No, definitely not. *Probably not*," he said with a little less confidence. "I scoured the apartment and got all of them. But that's what spooked me. The text was from her, and she was gloating about the fact that she was watching. I was too pissed to think straight, and, well, yeah."

"Well, yeah? What am I supposed to do with this? Tell you it's all good? No big deal, I do naked camera work all the time?"

He lowered his eyes. "I won't let anything like it happen again. I'm not going to make excuses for it. I knew Celia was fucked up, but I thought she had her limits. I know there are none anymore, and I'm going to stop her from screwing around with my life— with our lives—again."

I studied the ground while I tried to let everything digest. If I looked past the outrage of being filmed by some psychotic relative of Liam's, or the weirdness that his step-sister would set up spy cameras and watch him about to have sex, I could see that Liam wasn't the one to be upset with. I wasn't ready to just nod my head and trust that he was going to take care of this sister of his, though, or the potential video she had sitting on her computer of me butt naked getting eaten out.

"I want to talk to her," I said.

Liam flinched. Maybe it was my tone or something in my eye, but he was looking at me like I'd just said I was going to see if you could murder somebody with a spork. Yes, I might have been *wondering* if it was possible.

"That wouldn't be a good idea. Trust me. I'll do everything I can to stop her from interfering in our lives anymore. Until now, I was trying to lay low and avoid her. Not anymore. She crossed every goddamn line there is, and I'm done playing nice. I don't exactly know what I can do to get back at her, but if she doesn't back off, I'll figure something out."

I sighed. "If your plan for revenge is cruel enough, I'll let you handle it. But I think I have just as much reason to hate this woman as you do, so don't think I won't get involved if you're not doing a good enough job."

Some of the seriousness from his face finally drained. He grinned. "Remind me not to piss you off."

"Have a time machine?"

He chuckled. "Fair point."

"Besides, I'm still not sure I have forgiven you."

"Would pizza help?"

"A little bit. But you had better find a place with cheesy bread. And dessert pizza. And I need crab rangoons."

He scrunched up his forehead. "Are you sure you didn't mean all those 'and's to be 'or's?"

"I didn't stutter. Also, for questioning me, you also need to get a chocolate oreo milkshake with that."

He pursed his lips thoughtfully, then nodded. "Give me half an hour. You can fill me in on what I miss from the marathon. Also, you're hot when you get hardcore like that."

I scowled.

He just nodded and smirked. "Yep. That's the look."

I went inside, and once I was sure no one was watching, I smiled. I could be pissed about the video and his step-sister all I wanted. None of that meant I couldn't be happy that none of the things I'd assumed about Liam had been true last night. So I let the happiness come. I may have spent most of my life trying to convince everybody that I was practically allergic to happiness, but I was starting to think it was because I thought I'd never find it. After all, you can't fail to find what you don't look for.

Deep down, I was still scared it would come to an abrupt end. He'd turn out to be a jerk once the honeymoon phase of dating ended. Anyone could pretend to be nice for a couple dates or a few hours. None of the game-breaker bad habits or tendencies showed up that early, either. Maybe he was one of those animals who wore socks in bed, for example. Or maybe he didn't know how to brush his teeth without splattering the mirror with tiny specks of toothpaste. Worse, he could even drink skim milk.

Quirks aside, I could hardly imagine a future where things between us would work out. He'd probably get bored and break up with me, or maybe even cheat. He'd realize I was way too poor to be interesting for a guy like him. Or maybe he'd fail to stop his psychotic step-sister from ruining our relationship. Some way, it felt doomed.

And yet, stupid me still wanted to try.

10

LIAM

We abandoned the idea of actually watching the marathon of *Boy Meets World* about ten minutes after I arrived. I spent nearly thirty minutes in a state of awe as I watched Lilith and her seemingly bottomless appetite. She worked through three slices of pizza, four cheesy breadsticks, a slice of the dessert pizza, and three crab rangoons. She also polished off the entire milkshake.

"I feel a little emasculated here. I don't think I can even keep up with you." I set down the dessert pizza with a defeated sigh. The woman was half my size, and she'd outmatched me.

"It's not a competition," she said. "Unless you're a self-respecting man who doesn't want to be out-eaten by me, at least."

I laughed. "See, when you phrase it that way, it sounds a lot like a competition."

"It's okay to lose, Liam. Just embrace it."

"It's not even that. I'm just trying to figure out where you put it all."

"That's easy. I pre-fasted. I'm kind of a marathon junkie. I don't watch shows every day or even every week, but when I hear about a marathon coming on, I kind of make an event of it."

I grinned. "You realize Netflix is basically marathons on-demand, right? You don't have to wait for them to come on TV and watch commercials."

Something passed over her eyes that I couldn't quite read. "I think it's nostalgia. It's not the same without the commercials or the feeling that you have to plan your day around it. My parents were always riding me so hard about everything. But it was kind of a family tradition to do these marathon nights when their favorite shows were on. It was the one time they forgot to suck. We'd starve ourselves all day and then basically have a feast, then we watched as much as we could before we passed out. Maybe it was just the food coma, but those are probably my only memories with them when they weren't nagging me or pushing me. We just hung out and they didn't care if I was being perfectly ladylike."

I watched her face while she spoke, and I could almost see her when she was younger, sitting on the couch between two hard-faced parents. It made me realize how that little girl who had just wanted to feel accepted and loved was probably still inside her, and how she had learned to put on a tough face to convince the world she was okay.

I knew what she needed from me. She didn't need me to sweep her off her feet or to convince her she was the most beautiful girl in the world, even if I was starting to think she was. She just needed me to accept her and care about her. When I'd gone stiff after getting the text from Celia the other night, I'd probably shattered whatever trust she had been starting to put in me, and I'd have to work to rebuild it.

"So," I said. "I never stood a chance, because you've trained your whole life to eat like this?"

She nodded, and she even smiled. "Exactly."

Once Lilith had inhaled enough food, we sat on the couch. She let me put my arm around her and pull her in close to my chest. It felt good. I'd never been the cuddling type, maybe because I had never wanted to give women the wrong idea in the past, or maybe just because I'd never been interested enough in them in the first place.

"You know," Lilith said after a while. "In romance movies, when the guy and the girl pig out on pizza and then bang like ten minutes later, that's completely unrealistic. I mean, it's like you've got a greasy food baby in your stomach. Are you really thinking about stripping off your clothes, climbing on a guy, and trying to act like you feel sexy?"

"Greasy food baby," I repeated quietly. "You're right, I suddenly feel less in the mood when you put it that way."

She tilted her head to look up at me from where she was resting on my chest. "You don't think my food baby is sexy?" She lifted her shirt and pushed her stomach out so that it ballooned into a surprisingly round impression of early pregnancy.

I laughed, pressing my palm to her stomach softly and giving a playful squeeze. "I don't feel any food babies."

She squirmed away from my hands and sat up suddenly with a deadly serious look on her face. "Don't tickle me."

I raised my eyebrows. "What? Why not?"

"I'm not going to explain, so don't even try to ask why. Just don't do it."

"Come on. You can't leave me hanging with that. Why not?"

Her face went bright red. "Some women prefer to keep a few mysteries to themselves. Okay?"

I gave her a crooked smile. "Fine. But I'm going to find out one day. I guarantee it."

"I hope not. For both our sakes."

Lilith's phone was sitting on the armrest of the couch, and she barely caught it when it lit up and started vibrating its way toward the floor. She frowned at the screen. "Uh, shit," she said. "Sorry, do you mind if I take this? It might be the cat place"

I raised my eyebrows, but nodded. *The cat place?*

"Hello?" she said. I watched her face as she paused, then

frowned. "Oh. *Oh,* yeah. Claire. I remember you. From the thing at Galleon, sure."

Another pause.

"Um, sure. One second." She pulled the phone away from her ear and turned toward me. "Hey. Were you planning on doing anything with me tomorrow morning?"

"I have a few meetings tomorrow. I wasn't planning on continuing my seduction attempts until at least the evening."

She put the phone back to her ear. "Tomorrow morning is good."

She hung up a few seconds later. "That was this girl I met at a company party. She said she's having guy trouble or something and wanted to vent. I get free coffee, and I get juicy details about some drama."

"Well, if tonight goes according to plan, you'll need the caffeine."

"Why, are you going to drug me or something?"

"What? No. I meant I was going to have you out all night."

"Oh. Yeah. That makes more sense. But going out all night implies you'd make me miss the last four hours of this marathon. Your idea would have to be pretty badass to get me off this couch."

"Name it," I said. "If the city was yours for the taking, what would you want to do?"

"Uh, I don't know, sneak into Rockefeller center and ice skate after hours?"

"Easy. That's it?"

"Easy? I didn't take you for a rule breaker. The last sessions are at midnight. It's two in the morning, and they probably have security there."

"Leave it to me. Do you have skates?"

She got up wordlessly, opened a closet door, and pulled out a pair of relatively fancy looking ice skates. "Do you?"

. . .

THERE WAS ONLY ONE GUY WORKING SECURITY IN THE AREA, AND after a quick chat, it turned out that he was more than happy to let us sneak onto the ice for a hundred dollars. He even let me use a pair of rental skates. He looked more excited at the prospect of being bribed than by the actual amount I'd offered, and I suspected he would have agreed for five dollars, or even a cheeseburger.

I sat across from Lilith just outside the ice rink and started strapping on the skates. It was around that moment when I realized I'd never ice skated before, and I was very likely about to make an idiot of myself. "You sure this is what you want to do? I said you could do *anything*, remember?"

She stared at me, and then her lips slowly spread into a faint grin. "What you're trying to say is you don't know how to skate?"

"I wouldn't go *that* far. I don't have any first-hand experience, but how hard can it be?"

"We'll see, won't we?"

I yanked the straps tighter on my skates and decided I was going to kick this ice's ass. Lilith looked like she'd already decided I was going to embarrass myself, but I'd prove her wrong.

She stepped out onto the ice and clearly had plenty of practice, because she easily did a half-turn and started drifting backwards as she watched me with an eager expression. It almost looked like she *wanted* me to fall.

I steadied myself on the edge of the entrance gate and put my first tentative foot into the rink. The skate seemed to grip the ice well enough, and I let confidence surge through me. As soon as I lifted my back foot, my other foot slid forward on the ice and I did a split that I wasn't flexible enough for as I crashed down to the ground.

My crotch ignited with heat and a sharp kind of pain. I groaned and rolled to my side while I waited for the pain to subside.

Lilith came closer and reached down to help me up.

"I'm fine," I said. I couldn't manage to hide the strain from my voice as I gripped the gate and tried to hoist myself back to my feet.

"Try kind of splaying your feet out to the side so you won't slip forward like that," Lilith said.

"It's fine. The ice was just slick right there, and I—" My skates slid out from under me again, and this time I was flat on my back, staring up at Lilith as snow fell around her head. "I'd ask if you were an angel, but I don't think an angel would look so amused by my pain and suffering."

"I'm more amused by how stubborn you are. Do you want some help, or are you having fun busting your ass over and over?"

I awkwardly managed to scramble to a position on all fours, and then unsteadily straightened out. This time, I kept my skates under myself, but I could feel them threatening to slide out at any moment. All thoughts of looking cool and confident evaporated, and the only thing left was a primal need to survive this ordeal.

"I could maybe use some advice," I said without taking my eyes from my skates.

She glided up to me and put her small hands on my hips, steadying me. She tapped her hand on the inside of one of my thighs. "Try spreading your legs out a little more. If they're directly under you, the skates are going to want to go forward and back on their own."

"You know, I didn't think you'd be the one telling *me* to spread my legs tonight."

"Would you focus on not falling down instead of trying to make jokes?" She tapped my inner thigh again and pushed outward.

I let her guide my leg outward and immediately felt a little better. "Okay, so how do I go forward?"

"Just lean forward," she said.

I leaned forward and immediately lost balance. I flopped

down face-first on the ice, barely breaking my fall with my hands. I groaned.

Lilith laughed. "Oh my God. I didn't think you'd actually think that would work. I'm sorry. I feel bad for that one." She crouched down and helped me to stand back up. She was smiling wider than I'd ever seen, and any annoyance I felt couldn't stick when I saw how happy she seemed.

"Yeah, I guess I should've been able to figure out that was dumb."

"Which part, leaning forward or trusting me?"

"Both, probably."

She spent the next few minutes helping me get the basics down, and before long, I was making my way around the ice. It was pretty nice, and I forgot to care how goofy I must have looked moving at a fourth the speed she was. I spent my time watching her glide across the ice like it was her second home. She didn't do any spins or jumps to show off, but somehow I was sure she could have. After a while, she settled into a slow speed beside me.

"You're getting better," she said.

"Can't say I took you for an ice skater."

"Yeah, well, it's not like I was competing for the Olympics, or anything. It was just a guilty pleasure."

"Guilty? What's there to feel guilty about."

"My parents would've loved for me to like ice-skating. Anything that embodied girlishness and womanhood was an automatic 'yes' as far as they were concerned. Obviously there are male ice skaters, but, I mean... *Come on.*"

I grinned. "Yeah, the tight suits don't exactly scream macho. Or the jazz hands."

"Yeah, well, the fastest way to get me to hate something was for my parents to want me to do it. So ice skating was off the table. Or it should have been, at least. We went on a field trip as a class to ice skate once. I'd never tried it before, and I still remember how it felt that first time. Everything in my life was all rigidity and resistance. I was *always* fighting. Then I got on the ice and, for once, it felt like letting go. I knew I was doing something my parents would want, but that time, it was my choice."

I chuckled. "You know, you're kind of like a backwards version of Cinderella. The princess who wished she could be a commoner."

"If I'm backwards Cinderella, does that make you Prince Off-putting?"

"I'm too biased to answer. Why don't you tell me?"

She spun and skated backwards in front of me so she could grin at me. "Well, that depends. If you're put off by perfection and cockiness and ridiculous good looks. Then, yes. You definitely fit the bill."

"I'm hardly perfect."

She waited with raised eyebrows and took my hands, forcing me to come to a shaky stop beside her against the outer wall of the rink. "Prove it, asshole."

"There's your first bit of proof. There's no such thing as a perfect asshole. Honestly, who wants to look at that?"

"I'm serious. And thank you, by the way, considering you spread me out the other night and got a great look at my not-so-perfect asshole."

"I'm a gentleman. I'd never presume upon your asshole unless you offered it to me."

She burst out a surprised laugh and followed it with a smile that made me afraid I'd fall down again, but this time it would've had nothing to do with my lack of skating abilities.

"My asshole is safe unless I offer it to you," she mused. "Noted. Am I allowed to know what kind of ritual is involved when it comes to offering up my asshole to you?"

"Oh, you'll know when it's time."

"You still owe me proof, Mr. Off-putting.

"Okay. I'm not perfect because I like to dip my grilled cheese sandwiches in ketchup."

"Lame. I've totally done that. Have you ever bitten into a stick of butter like it was a candy bar?"

I cringed a little at the thought of that.

"Yeah, that's right. *Next.*"

"Okay," I said. "When I was eight, I clogged the toilet at my friend's house and blamed his grandma when they confronted me about it."

"You're a monster," she said dryly. "If this is all you have, I'm going to go ahead and assume you're still perfect."

"How about this. I think I'm falling for a girl I met a few days ago. It's absolutely a bad time in my life to get into a relationship. I've got too much going on at work to even consider dating. I've got a psychotic step-sister who is hell-bent on ruining my life and the life of anyone I care about. And she has a cat. Everybody knows cats are highly inferior to dogs, so she clearly has issues."

"A dog person. That confirms it. You're not perfect after all."

"So," I said as we started skating again. "You had to sneak around to practice this, I guess? Or did you eventually tell your parents?"

"I never told them. They still don't know. I used to lie and say I was staying after school to work on group projects. I'd come to the rink and zone out on the ice. It was when I'd daydream about who I would've been if my parents hadn't pushed so hard, I guess."

"And who would that have been?"

She gave me a crooked smile. "Some goody-two-shoes prissy girl, probably." She shrugged. "Maybe it's a good thing they tried so hard to make me into what they wanted. After all, you don't seem like the type to go after princesses."

I laughed. "It only took one to realize it wasn't my style. No, I like somebody with backbone. You're different, and I like that about you."

"You're different than I thought you'd be too. I have to admit, I had you pegged as a guy named Kade who spent all day on his yacht."

I laughed. "Well, one of my best friends is named Kade, unfortunately. And I may or may not technically own a yacht. So maybe I'm not so different, after all."

She laughed. "Where there's money, there's a Kade. It's like a universal law. Do you have a friend named Rich, too? Or maybe *Edward*?"

"Not Rich, but my step brother's name *is* Price."

"Damn! I could win a game of rich person cliché bingo with you in seconds."

"I can play the game too," I said. "Do you make sacrifices on Halloween? Do you like to go into the woods at night and dance around campfires naked?"

"No and yes," she said with a completely straight face.

"Wasn't expecting a yes, but maybe if you just want to shoot me a text before your next nude forest dance, I can watch and give you pointers on your technique."

"You'd like that, wouldn't you? *Perv*."

"I did strip you down and spell the alphabet between your legs with my tongue last night. Clearly I'm interested in what's under your clothes. I didn't think I was making a secret of that."

She blushed. "Yeah, well, at least my imperfect asshole is still a secret. I guess."

"Definitely didn't look. For long."

She tried to swat at me, but I caught her hands. "As far as assholes go, yours was spectacular."

"Stop it. You're going to make me blush, and I don't blush."

"You're already blushing."

"No, that's just internal bleeding of my face. Don't flatter yourself."

"My mistake. I thought maybe my seduction was finally starting to work."

"Maybe just a little."

"Either way. I'm glad tonight happened. I liked getting to see behind the curtains, even if only a bit."

"And what do you see behind my curtains?" she asked.

"I'm not sure. My eyes were closed when I went down there."

She paused, then grimace in disgust. "Oh my God. Please never call any part of female anatomy "curtains" again."

I laughed. "I'm sorry. Completely agree it's a horrible and unflattering word. But I couldn't resist. You practically gave me a layup there."

She raised her eyebrows and spread her hands out wide. "So? Your terrible sense of humor aside. What secrets did I reveal to you?"

"That maybe you have a little bit of an excuse for being such a cold bitch all the time."

She laughed. "Just say how you feel. *Damn.*"

"I'm mostly kidding. You put up a good front, but I never really bought the act. Not entirely."

"Who says it's an act?"

"Your eyes do. You can control your face pretty well, but not your eyes. And the way your mouth twitches when you think something's funny. That, and the way you've been eye-fucking me since the first time we met."

She opened her mouth to protest and then clamped it shut.

I barked a laugh. "Damn. Was I that spot on?"

"Shut up. No. I just couldn't believe how cocky you sounded."

"But was I wrong?"

"I wasn't *eye-fucking* you. I would sometimes imagine what you were like, maybe. But that's as far as it went."

"For someone who spends all day pretending, you're a bad liar."

"You're skating on thin ice, *Bob.*"

I looked down. "What? This is solid"

She rolled her eyes. "Poor choice of words. You know what I

mean. If you want all these romantic gestures of yours to pay off, you might want to stop teasing me."

"I have no idea what you're talking about. I'm not making romantic gestures, and I'm not hoping for some kind of payoff."

"We're ice skating together while snowflakes are drifting down around us. Come on. This is a maximum effort romantic gesture. Ninety percent effort at the least. Just admit it. You're trying hard, even if I can't figure out why you're interested in me in the first place."

"More like a hundred and ten," I admitted with a chuckle. "I'm trying so hard because I can't help it. I don't understand it completely, but I know it feels different with you. From the moment we first talked, I felt drawn in. I went from never thinking about anything but work to having to force myself to focus when I was working. I couldn't stop running through scenarios of how I could win you over or break through those barriers of sarcasm you put up."

"Barriers of sarcasm. Ouch."

"I wasn't complaining."

"So why haven't you asked the important question yet?"

I turned to face her, forgetting I was on skates, and promptly busted my ass.

To add to the humiliation, I continued sliding for a few feet on my butt before my back bumped against the outer barrier of the rink.

Lilith gracefully went down to her knees and slid up to me until she was squatted right between my legs, eyes intent on mine. The sudden silence of the night without the scrape of our skates on the ice felt startling.

"I think I've hit my head too many times tonight to figure out the important question," I said. "Maybe you can help me out."

"You haven't asked why I've agreed to go on two dates with you."

"Isn't it obvious?" I asked with a grin.

She punched my chest, drawing a laugh from me. "I'm serious."

I let the smile fade from my mouth and shook my head. "Do I have to make the correct guess, or is this a rhetorical question?"

"I've agreed to go on dates with you because normally, people wear me out. A few minutes of social interaction and I'm ready to call it a week. You're the first guy I've ever wanted more from." She let her eyes fall, and the silence that followed seemed to add more weight to her words.

I reached up to touch her chin, tilting her face up toward mine. "This is the part where I'd normally make some kind of move, but I don't actually think I can move more than my arms without falling down even more."

"What are you saying?"

"I'm going to need you to just drag me out of here and then forget it ever happened, if you want this to go further, at least."

She got to her feet, stepped to my side, and took both my hands. She pushed off and started pulling me across the ice on my back.

"Your ass looks nice from down here," I said as I stared up at her.

She turned and glared. "You're saying it doesn't look nice from your normal vantage point?"

"Not at all. Just that it's great from every angle."

"Yeah, I wonder if your step-sister agrees."

I winced a little at that. It was fair, even if I hated what Celia had done just as much as Lilith must.

She dragged me up to the gate and I was able to plant my hands and shimmy off the ice in a highly undignified way. "I think I enjoyed getting dragged across the ice more than skating on it."

"Because of my ass, or because you weren't at risk of falling?"

"Definitely the ass."

She bit her lip, then knelt down and started pushing against my shoulders. I was still sitting down, and for a second I thought she was trying to get me to lay back down on my back.

"What are you doing?"

"I want you just how you were back there. Yeah," she said, nudging my legs a little until I opened them up. "That looks right." She knelt down between my legs again, just like she was a minute ago on the ice. "You were saying if you could move properly you'd make a move, if I recall."

I took the back of her neck and pulled her down to kiss me. Her lips were a little cold, but her tongue felt white-hot. Distantly, I hoped the security guard I'd bribed hadn't stuck around where he could catch a view of us making out, but I also wasn't about to let anything stop me from taking her the way I wanted this time. Not again.

"Are you sure she isn't filming this?" Lilith asked.

"No," I admitted. "But I'd be pretty impressed if she had thought to hide cameras here. I was planning on taking this inside, though. Frostbite on your ass isn't exactly my idea of a great finale to the night."

11

LILITH

By the time we forced our way into one of the glassed-off shops beside the skating rink, we were both in our socks, my shirt was half-way undone, and Liam's pants were unbuttoned. We had kiss-walked our way toward the door, tearing at clothes and the ice-skates with whatever brain cells we could spare.

I licked my lips. "Hypothetically speaking, what happens if I let you have me?"

"What happens is I lay you down, stand you up, or hold you sideways—doesn't matter—I spread you out. I dive into you like it has been years instead of days since I first decided I wanted to fuck you. I *had* to fuck you. You say the word, and I'll devour you. Every last goddamn inch. That's what happens."

I tried to swallow but only produced an awkward clicking noise in my throat. *Damn.* He was hot when he was horny. "Hypothetically, of course," I said quietly. "That sounds like a little more fun than seven point two inches of silicone."

"Hypothetically," he agreed.

Two minutes later, Liam had me pressed against a wall behind a door marked "Staff Only." It had turned out to be a kind of maintenance room, and we could hear the sound of the security officer watching some laugh-track sitcom through the thin walls.

His hand pinned my wrists over my head and his face was inches from mine. Every nerve in my body screamed for his touch until my skin felt like glitter, prickling all over. I could worry about consequences and implications later. From the moment I saw him, whether I wanted to admit it to myself or not, I'd been on a collision course with Liam Hightower. He cut straight through all the attempts I made at showing the world I didn't care. When it came to him, I cared. A lot.

I wanted what he had to give, and I wanted it so badly it hurt. It hadn't been a matter of *if*, but *when*.

He kissed me in that hard, possessive way of his, like every touch of his lips was a mark to show the world that I had been claimed and they had better stay away.

"What are we doing?" I asked between kisses.

"This is called foreplay," he said slowly, like he was explaining something to a child. "First I get you so horny you can barely stand, then I—"

"I understand the concept," I interrupted. "What is this? What does it mean?"

He shrugged. "It doesn't have to mean anything. For once, stop trying to assign meaning to everything. Just experience it. Live it. Deal with the questions later."

His words washed over me, hardly sinking into my mind because I was so preoccupied with his closeness. His body was hard against mine, warm and full of delicious promise. His length was rock-hard and pressing into my stomach, giving me no doubt where *he* wanted this night to go.

"What if it's not that simple?"

He leaned forward, taking my lower lip between his teeth and pulled away slowly, leaving me with a slight sting and a burning hunger for more. "What if it is?"

I tried to channel some of his nonchalance. This wasn't high school anymore. People did have casual sex. Casual relationships. Sometimes the lines didn't have to be black and white. Couldn't I just step into that world this one time?

Liam put his hand on the inside of my thigh, yanking my thoughts away from any doubts I had and bringing them straight to the neon sign flashing in my mind that said "Do it."

So I let go. I relaxed my body, letting his hand swallow up my wrists and letting his other hand burn a trail up the inside of my thigh. I let him slide my pants down and then I let him cup me between the legs, his skin hot against my already-soaked panties.

He kissed my earlobe. "Your pussy doesn't seem to be having doubts."

"That was never the part of me you had to fight to win over," I admitted. "You had me between the legs from the first glance. It was the rest of me that wasn't ready to admit it."

"*Fuck,*" he rasped, fingers moving slowly and rhythmically against me. "I knew you were dirty from the first moment I saw you. You hid it well, but I knew. I could see you wishing for it in the apartment lobby, wishing I'd make a move."

"I don't see—*oh God*—how you would've thought that."

He squeezed my wrists harder, lips still so close to my ear that I could feel them move as he spoke, as his fingers snuck up to the waistband of my panties and dove inside, spreading my slick arousal along his fingers. "You were eye-fucking me from the first time you saw me. Admit it."

"Liar," I said.

He chuckled, and I felt the sound vibrating through his chest to mine. "I'm a lot of things, but I've never been a liar."

I almost argued with him—pointed out that he'd been far from honest when he introduced himself under a fake name—but the sensations flooding me were too much to think, too much to speak. The only sounds that came from my mouth were unintelligible, moans so loud I hoped the security guard couldn't hear it over his TV show.

He finger-fucked me so hard I came while shaking and holding on to him to keep from falling down. My knees were like jelly, my brain like scrambled eggs as some distant, logical part of me was still trying to grapple with what this moment meant, what it implied about our future or lack thereof.

He sank to one knee like he was about to propose, then looked up at me with a wolfish grin. He held up his forefinger and middle finger, which were slick with my juices. Without looking away from me, he ran his tongue up them from base to tip, drinking me in. He bit his lip and his grin widened. "Fuck you taste good. I need more." He yanked my panties down in a quick motion, pulled them off of me completely, and then hooked his arms under my legs, dropping me down until my back was against the wall and my weight was on his shoulders. There was no time to think, no time to doubt or question.

"You have the sexiest pussy I've ever seen," he growled before he kissed the insides of my thighs. His face was so close to my sex that I could feel the heat radiating from his skin like a lingering promise of what was coming. I felt like I should be embarrassed or self-conscious, because it was much brighter in here than it had been in his apartment at night, but all I could feel was anticipation.

When he put his lips to me, it was like time stopped. The warmth of his tongue in such an intimate place almost pushed me to climax instantaneously. I thought of all the wicked things that tongue had helped him orchestrate, and how watching him use it to please me felt so deliciously naughty. I hadn't expected the sense of power to be so sexy.

He pulled my clit between his lips, circling it with his tongue before plunging it inside me and tongue-fucking me. It was too much, and I clenched around him, scissoring his head between my thighs when the orgasm came barreling through me like a freight train.

He eased me off his shoulders, and set me down on the ground before stripping out of his remaining clothes. He quickly peeled a condom from its wrapper and slid it down his erect length.

He got to his knees, grabbed me by the legs, and pulled me toward him until his cock laid between my legs and he was looking down at me with heavy-lidded eyes.

I wanted to do the dainty thing and wait for him to put himself inside me, but the bastard seemed like he was going to just stay there, roaming my body with his eyes. Taking things into my own hands, I reached out for him and guided him inside me. I was soaked already, and he slid right in.

I laid back and reached above my head to hook my fingers underneath the closed door and hooked my legs around his back, spreading myself so he could drive himself deeper and deeper, until I thought it wasn't possible for him to fill me any more fully.

"You feel so good," I gasped.

"You're surprised?"

"Asshole," I said, trying to laugh but losing the sound when he ripped another moan from me. I'd never been the loud type before, but it was impossible not to be loud with Liam. He had a way of making me feel like I was in a movie or a fairy tale. He wanted to take me for his own, and bit by bit, I realized that I wanted that, too. I wanted to be tangled up with him, part of his life and his world. I wanted to curl myself up in his heart and make my bed there.

My thoughts were soon blasted away by his increasing pace. I watched his expression, loving the way his beautiful features twisted with raw pleasure. He gripped my hips, and the last of the delicate, slow way he had been taking me was obliterated when he started using my hips like handles, slamming me into himself like a fuck toy. *God it was so hot.*

The line between orgasms blurred. I wasn't even sure if I was about to climax, in the middle of one, or coming down from one. All I knew was if the kiss had felt right, this *was* right. Sex like this didn't exist between people who weren't meant to be together. I believed that. I had to believe that.

He groaned, collapsing onto me as he came.

"Fuck," he gasped into my chest. "I was planning on lasting a lot longer than that."

I laughed, but the sound was weak. My body was still convulsing all over, skin ablaze with pleasant waves of bliss. "Fortunately for you, it's quality, not quantity that counts. I'm starting to reconsider my stance on the merits of sex toys versus the real thing."

"Dork," he laughed.

I slapped at his chest, but bit my lip and smiled. "It's rude to call someone a dork while you're balls deep inside them."

He leaned down and kissed my chin while grinning wickedly. "I want to hear you admit you'd do anything for more of this." He moved his hips in a subtle little thrust that immediately re-ignited all the heat in my stomach.

"I'll do no such thing."

"Too bad. I guess I'll just pull it out then."

I sat up and gripped his tight ass, holding him inside me. "No. You won't."

"Damn, it's kind of hot when you get all bossy on me."

"Good. Then you won't mind when I order you to do it again. Just like the last time." I leaned back and looked up at him with an expression that probably wasn't as menacing as I wanted since I couldn't stop from smirking.

He gave a quick salute and nodded. "I should warn you. I'm an overachiever, so I hope you weren't planning on making it to work tomorrow morning."

12

LIAM

Price and Kade were already waiting for me outside my office. I tried to look alert, but I was running on about one hour of sleep, and even that had been invaded by a particularly enjoyable dream involving Lilith.

Price, as usual, elected for the business-very-casual look. He sported a button-down shirt with the sleeves rolled up. At least it looked like he had combed his wild hair, which wasn't always a given. For some reason, women seemed to eat his lazy, carefree style up, even if I would've preferred some more professionalism when he was on the company clock, I couldn't complain. Price got the job done and done well in his uniquely frustrating way.

Kade loomed like a statue by the door, as if he'd been placed there to frighten off anyone who might think about coming in my office.

"To what do I owe the honor?" I asked. "It's not like you two to make a house call."

"Opportunity is knocking," Price said. He opened my door for me and gestured for me to enter.

Kade, oblivious as always, walked right in front of me as if Price had opened the door for him.

I settled in behind my desk, where I had to resist the urge to log in to my computer and start checking emails right away. Multi-tasking had never been a speciality of mine. I was prone to tunnel vision on every level of my life. If I had four tasks for the day, I'd often get so fixated on completing the first to absolute perfection that I'd only realize I had left no time for the remaining three when it was too late. On a larger scale, I'd fixated on landing the career I wanted all through school at the expense of having a social life. Once I started the company, I had continued to ignore everything but work. If I hadn't taken on the Bob Smith persona to avoid my step-sister, I wasn't sure I would have ever felt I had the time to spare to date again.

I wondered if Lilith had any idea how much trouble she was in by becoming my latest fixation. Worse, I wondered if I would even be able to keep my life on track when all I wanted to do was see more of her, to *taste* more of her.

I clenched my hands tightly around the armrests of my chair. I knew Price was talking, but all I could hear were the soft, desperate breaths of Lilith as I worked into her and drove her to ecstasy. It was hard to imagine wanting or caring about anything else, like I'd just had my first real hit of a drug I knew was going to consume me. The frightening part was that I was absolutely ready to let her take me over, even when I wasn't sure how my life could come crashing down around us.

"So?" Price asked.

"He was zoned out," Kade said. "Speaking from experience on that. Didn't hear a word you said, I guarantee it."

"I was absolutely listening," I said.

"Then give me the plagiarized high-school essay version of what I just said."

"You... were telling me about a business opportunity."

Price sighed. "No, asshole. I was telling you I had to get an endoscopy because I couldn't take a shit for three days and I was getting worried."

I raised an eyebrow. "What?"

"Yeah. Turned out it was just this new protein shake I was trying. Not enough veggies or something. Fiber, all that kind of stuff."

Kade nodded wisely. "Fiber is important. Helps keep you regular. Yogurt is good too. Good bacteria for your gut, but if you have lactose problems like me, you can always go with the probiotic route."

"Is this seriously why you two waited outside my office? My bowel movements are perfectly fine, thank you."

"No," Price said. "It's called small talk. Normal people do it before they talk business with their friends."

"Actually," Kade said. "I don't know how normal it is to talk about that kind of stuff. It's funny. We all do it, but everybody wants to sweep it under the rug like having a bowel movement is a big conspiracy." He chuckled and shook his head. "Sometimes you just want to come out and scream it at the top of your lungs, you know? 'Hey! I shit! And I'm proud of it!'"

Price and I sighed at the same time.

"Kade," Price said. "You're the weirdest man I've ever met. There's a reason we don't let you meet clients, and that comment was a prime example."

Kade pointed at Price while he looked to me with raised brows. "See what I mean? He wants to sweep me right under the rug because I talked about it."

"Whatever you say, Kade," Price said. "The real reason we came by was to tell you that we've got a big fish on the line. She's the liaison for a multinational corporation, and they have a juicy stock package they give to all their higher-ups. If they incorporated our packages to their compensation programs, we'd be looking at close to double what we're pulling in now, just like that. Think about it. One deal, and double everything, maybe more. Because who knows what a big ass company like that could do for our reputation."

"So you're saying we would make a lot of money from them." I spread my hands. "But if there wasn't a catch, you wouldn't be trying so hard to convince me this was a good thing."

"A small catch," Price admitted. "I know you prefer me to do all the wheeling and dealing for you, but this lady wants to meet with you personally. She said she doesn't want the sales pitch. She wants to see straight into the mind behind these packages. Control freak, I guess."

"I see. Figure out the details of what she's expecting and get back to me. I'm not taking her to baseball games or something ridiculous. We can have a meeting in a professional setting. I'll bring my laptop and run her through the process. But I'm not doing more than that. No bullshit cartwheels or powerpoints."

"People like powerpoints," Kade said. "Think about it. When you were in school, the day your teacher pulled out a powerpoint was the best. Next to watching a movie, at least."

Price and I both looked at Kade like he was an idiot, which, in all likelihood, he really was.

Price turned back to look at me. "Not even a little persuasion? Your anti-social grunting techniques aren't going to work here. This is a big payday. Not just for you, either. Think about all our employees. The guy who works the front desk. The secretaries. The grunts who plug in the numbers. My team who busts their asses every day to scout new clients. Think about it, man. All that rides on you gripping those big balls of yours and pretending you know how to be persuasive."

"Come on, Price," I said. "I know you well enough to know you don't care about the employees, so don't pretend you do."

"But you do." He pointed at me and gave an obnoxiously knowing grin. "There's a reason I'm a good salesman, Liam. It's because I can figure out people on the fly. I can hit them where it matters. I've known you way too fucking long to need to figure anything out, so just give up before I have to pull out the big guns and *really* start getting persuasive."

I chuckled and shook my head. "Fine. But I'm not agreeing because I think you can persuade me. I'm agreeing because you're so stubborn that I know you'll bore me into submission if I try to resist."

He reached across my desk and patted my shoulder. "That's the spirit."

13

LILITH

I met Claire at a coffee shop near my apartment. I hadn't actually seen her since the night at Galleon when I was manning the front desk on William's orders. I hadn't actually expected to see the woman again. I'd lost count of how many times a casual acquaintance had said the fateful, "we should totally hang out sometime." Of course, "sometime" was another way to say hypothetically. It was more like saying, "I don't ever plan to rearrange my life to make time to be your friend, but hypothetically, if I was willing to do that, I'm sure we'd have fun." So when Claire had taken my number back at Galleon, the last thing I expected was to get a phone call from her.

Claire sipped her coffee, eying me over the brim of her cup. With that black hair and widow's peak, I found myself a little jealous of her natural villain look. I put a lot of effort into making myself look like somebody you would be hesitant to approach, but Claire seemed like my polar opposite. She was naturally gifted with mischievous, frightening eyes and a twist to her mouth that made it look like she'd just finished whispering lies about you. Yet she dressed in bright colors and an outfit that seemed to scream to the world that she was sweet and innocent.

Then there was me. I had spent most of my childhood being told I looked like a princess. I was groomed to *be* a modern-day princess. Some dolled up enigma designed and engineered to snare a wealthy man. I pushed back the whole way, but the ghosts of that expectation were never far from my mind.

Every morning, I did my best to cover that memory up with makeup and a practiced expression of indifference. I didn't want to look like a princess. I didn't want to be a princess. I wanted to be me, but even I didn't know who that was anymore.

"Surprised you came," Claire said.

I came about five times before I lost count last night. The dirty little voice in my head hadn't stopped connecting everything to last night with Liam. It was worse than a middle schooler who had just discovered the power of "that's what she said" and couldn't stop compulsively using it after every sentence. I had to force an awkward smile and think about black and white baseball to calm down the growing heat in my stomach. The man had been like electricity, and ever since he put his hands on me last night, he'd turned something on that I didn't know how to shut off.

"Yeah," I said quietly. I cleared my throat. "You seemed kind of cool, so."

She shrugged. "I'm not cool at all. Honestly, I wanted to come clean with you. I had a big falling out with my friends, and I am pretty much desperate for some human contact lately. Even waiting a few days to call you was like pulling teeth. I just didn't want to creep you out and seem too desperate."

"Too late. I'm creeped out."

She laughed. "Sorry. I thought I could just tell you were someone I'd get along with. It's always so weird trying to make friends as an adult. It's like asking someone on a date, practically."

"If I'd known this was a date, I would've brought my cleavage."

She looked at me with a mischievous grin and flicked open one button on her shirt. "I came prepared to adapt."

"So, you said you had a falling out with your friends?" I wanted to change the subject, because for a minute, I wasn't sure if the woman was actually trying to hit on me. I didn't have anything against girls who were into the whole rug burn thing, but it wasn't my style, and I didn't want to give her the wrong idea.

Her gaze sank to the table. "Yeah. I did something stupid. I misread somebody, and I really pissed him off. And then I made it worse by kind of trying to get him back for embarrassing me. Basically, all my friends hate me now."

"Did you try apologizing?"

Her eyes flicked back to mine, and I saw a startling determination there. "I'm not the apologizing type. I tend to double down, even when I'm in the wrong." She laughed, and all the fierce intensity in her expression was gone again. "Sorry. This is exactly how you scare away potential friends. I guess it's good that you get to see the real me, warts and all. Right?"

After coffee with Claire, I headed to work. It admittedly felt kind of good to have some normal girl talk. My best friend had been out of the country for months, and she had been my only source of female drama. Of course, I'd always pretended to hate it when Emily unloaded her drama and vented to me, but I think it secretly scratched an itch.

Claire ended up asking me about my love life, and oddly enough, I'd felt like sharing. I didn't go into much detail, but talking about how unexpected my new love interest had been and my feelings for him was strangely therapeutic. Talking to Claire actually helped me sort through my feelings about Liam and how I hoped our relationship would develop. Go figure. Maybe the girl-talk ritual had some practical use, after all.

Even at work, my mind went straight back to Liam. So much so that I'd forgotten about William's stupid little birthday party that night. Of course, William didn't let me forget it when I got to work, and neither did Grammy, who had, unfortunately, decided she was going to hang around Galleon until the birthday preparations were set up to her expectations. She'd even wheeled over one of the intern's chairs to my desk and made it her second home, complete with the knitting magazines that she spread over my keyboard, even though I knew for a fact she didn't knit.

"Can you maybe *not* sit so close to me? You smell like a retirement home," I asked. She actually didn't smell, but the only thing that made the woman tolerable was if you kept her on her feet by insulting her first. She'd never admit it, but she enjoyed the back and forth. I might have kind of enjoyed it a little, too.

"Maybe because I live in one, dipshit," Grammy snapped.

"It's called a shower," William said. He had popped out of his office and leaned on my desk in the middle of our exchange.

"I'm sure I know more about showers than you know about combs," She said. "Look at that ridiculous hair. It looks like you drove to work with your head out the goddamn window. It's just too bad you didn't high-five a street sign with your teeth."

I snorted. Grammy could be savage, especially when it came to William. The pair had an ever-escalating insult war that seemed to forever wage on between them.

William smirked. His hair *was* kind of crazy, but he had the type of face that meant it didn't matter. I still enjoyed seeing Grammy give him hell. "I gave you a ride to work. Why the hell do you think I stuck my head out the window? *Shower. You should try it.*"

She tried to hide it, but I saw a smile threatening to spread her lips. "If skipping a shower means you'll stick your dumbass head out the window for the whole car ride, then I'll have them shut the damn water off in my room."

"You're the one who insisted on me giving you a ride. I offered to pay for an Uber."

"I don't want your dirty money, pencil dick."

He threw his hands up in frustration. "I've told you so many fucking times. Pencils come in all sizes and shapes. That's not even a good insult. This guy used to come do SAT prep in high school, and he carried a prop pencil with him that was five feet tall and a foot thick."

"Is your ass jealous?" Grammy asked. "Because so much shit is coming out of your mouth, it must be wondering if it's getting laid off."

William tried to fight it but finally chuckled. "Shitbag," he murmured before stalking back to his office.

It was a pretty typical exchange between the two of them. They'd trade insults until somebody unofficially won. Usually, Grammy won through pure stubbornness and refusal to quit.

"He's a good kid," she said.

"You ever tell him that?" I asked.

She made a dismissive noise. "You think I'm going to tell the man who thinks he's God's gift to the Earth that I like him? Hell no. Maybe on my deathbed. *Maybe.*"

"I thought you weren't planning on ever dying?"

"Exactly."

I grinned. "Fair point."

"So, when are you going to spill the beans? I can smell dick on you. You got laid, and you're not telling me."

"Please tell me that's just a figure of speech." I lifted my armpit and sniffed, but all I could smell was a faint hint of my deodorant."

"You know what they say, once a hoe has the scent of dick in her nose, she can smell it from a mile away, even in the water."

I scrunched up my face. "What? No. Nobody says that, Grammy. I think you just mixed together like three real facts into some special brand of bullshit."

"I know you got laid because I know. One day, when you've lived to be as well-aged and dignified as me, you'll understand that young people aren't nearly as sneaky as they think they are. You turds wear your feelings on your face, and I can read you like a book."

"Then why do I need to spill the beans if you already know?"

"Listen, you little shit. You're going to tell me what happened, how long it took, how big he was, and what dirty little things he whispered in your ear. You're going to tell me willingly, or I'm going to psychologically torture it out of you."

"You mean you're going to be your normal self? How is that even a threat?"

"You haven't even begun to see the depths of what I'm capable of, Lilith. I could make a grown man cry with nothing but six words."

"Good thing I'm not a grown man, I guess."

Grammy raised her eyebrows at the challenge.

As it turned out, I only lasted two minutes against her methods before I spilled everything.

LIAM MET ME AT GALLEON THAT NIGHT FOR WILLIAM'S SURPRISE birthday party. Everyone who came for the party met on the 36th floor, and we'd finally convinced Hailey to invite William to "secretly" meet her there for a little clandestine husband and wife bangery.

Liam's business partners, Price and Kade, had come along. Price looked like what every used car salesman imagined they looked like. Sauve, rugged, and dripping with charm. He had a sharp nose with piercing brown eyes, and he looked like he'd taken a page from William's book on casual fashion.

Kade was what I imagined a statue would look like if it woke up one day and became spontaneously sentient. He looked like he could've dunked a basketball by standing on his tiptoes, and he had a face that vaguely reminded me of a young Arnold Schwarzenegger.

Price shook my hand and looked at Liam with raised brows. "So *this* was your type all along? No wonder you never hit it off with those girls I set you up with."

"What type am I, exactly?" I asked him.

He flinched back at my tone, then laughed and waggled his finger at me. "That's good. She's good, Liam. Scary, but with that little edge of sexy. Yeah, I can see why you like her."

"You look like the kind of man who would scream like a girl if he got stabbed." I leaned a little closer. "Want to prove me wrong?"

He did a full body shiver and shook his hands out, laughing a little nervously as he looked between me and Liam. "Jesus, man. Did you get her as a guard dog, or a girlfriend? I can't tell which."

"Lilith has a low tolerance for bullshit," Liam said. "So you might want to avoid speaking near her.

"You know," Kade said. "I used to have a this thing with lettuce. If I saw lettuce or especially if I *heard* the sound of lettuce leaves crunching around, my lip would curl up kind of Elvis style. I couldn't help it. Especially if it was kind of papery lettuce, that was the worst. Crazy thing was, I love lettuce. Always have. I just had to look like the King while I was eating it."

Price was staring at Kade with furrowed eyebrows. "You're about five sentences past the part where this should have started having some relevance to what we're talking about."

"I was going to say if she's got an issue with bullshit, she could try what I did. My therapist just kept exposing me to more and more lettuce, bit by bit. He even had me listen to the sound in headphones while I watched my mouth in a mirror. Eventually, I got over it."

"Great," I said. "So we put Price's voice in some headphones, have me sit in a quiet room, and eventually I won't want to hurt things from the sound of it?"

"That's the basic idea," Kade said. "Yep."

"The basic idea is that you're an idiot," Price said.

"Just because I'm big, it doesn't mean I don't have feelings that can be hurt."

Liam put his hand to his mouth to cover a smile. "They're special. I know."

Kade and Price lost track of us as they descended into a back-and-forth argument over who was truly the stupid one.

"I can't judge. My friends are idiots, too." I gestured toward Grammy, who was pulling down her sweatpants to show a crowd of well-dressed businessmen the top of her leopard-print thong.

"Woah," said Liam. "Is that kind of like a stripper you get as a gag?"

"That's the birthday boy's grandmother-in-law."

Liam choked back a laugh. "I see."

Grammy noticed us looking at her and headed for us.

"Oh shit. She sees us."

"Is that bad?" asked Liam.

"You'll see."

Grammy slid her glasses down to look at Liam. She didn't make any attempt to hide that she was clearly checking him out from head to toe and liking what she saw. "Well, well, well. She was right about you. You *do* look like you'd have a huge cock."

I cringed. Grammy's psychological torture had been particularly effective, and I hadn't been given the option to hold back any detail, including the size of his penis, roughly speaking, at least. I wasn't sure what reaction I expected, but when Liam turned to me with a grin, I was relieved. "Considering your expertise in dildos and the effectiveness of varying sizes, I'll consider that a compliment. I'm sure you've had bigger, after all," he said.

I no longer even tried to lie to myself about the heat in my cheeks around Liam. I was definitely blushing. "This is Grammy," I said quickly. "She should probably be getting ready to lie down, so she doesn't die of exertion or something. Shouldn't she?"

"Your life expectancy is going to be a hell of a lot shorter than mine if you try to shoo me away from this hunk of man meat, bubble tits."

"Bubble tits? Seriously?" I asked.

"Look at those things. I've never seen such circular boobs before. You need to teach those puppies to sag a little like a real woman's."

"Grammy," I said under my breath. "I don't know Liam well enough for you to be this weird in front of him. You're going to scare him off."

Liam leaned forward and lowered his voice to match mine. "I can hear everything you're saying, and nothing is going to scare me off, not even your bubble tits."

I slapped his arm, but he only grinned.

"I happen to like them just the way they are. And I'm sure I'd like them if gravity decided to start paying attention to them."

Grammy nodded. "Told you. Men like a little sag. They want the weight of a boob in their hands. Give them a good two-pounder and they'll cum on the spot."

"Grammy!" I snapped. "Just go, please. Don't you have strippers to prepare for when William gets here?"

She made a dismissive sound. "I'll leave, but only because I'm bored of you. *Not you, hunkie*," she said before pinching Liam's cheek.

"I like her," he said.

"Ugh. You have bad taste, then."

"I must, because I like you too."

"Yeah. See? You're obviously an idiot." I couldn't stop myself from smiling anyway. He was looking at me with a glint in his eye, and it was doing a bunch of dumb, girly things to my body.

"Wow," Liam said. "Is that a stripper?"

I laughed out loud when I saw William standing in the elevator with a surprised look on his face. He was butt naked except for generous amounts of whipped cream on his nipples and between his legs. He even had a cherry buried in the whipped cream on his right nipple, but the cherry on his left had either been eaten or fallen off.

His entrance was met with stunned silence. Hailey put her hand to her face and hung her head in shame as a slow-forming smile spread William's lips. "Wow, Hailey," he said. "You invited me up here for a little bangaroo, and you brought this many people to watch? You kinky little vixen."

"William," she said in a warning voice. "It's a surprise party. For your *birthday*."

"Oh, I know. Grammy left a receipt for strippers on my desk. She also had Lilith send out an email to some people in the office, and I knew you guys would plan something, so I was snooping through all the outgoing messages."

Bruce stepped forward with a look on his face that was somehow both surprised, but not surprised, or maybe it was that he was rotating back and forth between the two emotions. "You knew we'd all be waiting here and you came up wearing *that*?"

"Surprise?" he asked.

Hailey moved toward him and pushed him back into the elevator. He was so much bigger than her that seeing the small woman shoving the naked mountain of muscle back into the elevator was comical. William gave a quick wave and a smile before the elevator doors closed.

"He's dumber than I thought," Grammy said. "But he looks good in whipped cream. I'll give him that."

"That was your boss?" Liam asked.

"Unfortunately."

"He normally wears more than that to work, right?"

"Why, are you jealous?" I asked, wiggling my eyebrows.

He didn't answer, but his eyes lingered on the elevator doors. A tingle of warmth rushed up my spine at the look on his face. I felt possessed, but in an oddly pleasant way. I saw in his features that he'd already claimed me as his own, *marked* me. He didn't care how minor the threat was, and he wasn't going to whine about it, but he was also going to be watching William like a hawk from now on.

A few minutes later, William came back in a sweatshirt and sweatpants. He was grinning like an idiot, and Hailey was following closely behind him with her cheeks flushed red.

"Hailey," I said, catching her by the arm as she headed back into the party. "You've got whipped cream on your mouth. *Harlot.*"

She put her hand to her lips and rubbed away the smear of white on her bottom lip. Her already-red cheeks grew even darker. "Thank you," she murmured before fast-walking to catch up with William.

Liam and I were both distracted by the parade of half-naked men that poured out of the elevator a few minutes later. Each of them wore nothing but neon yellow underwear. My eyes went past the men to Claire, who was leaning against the railing of the stairs. She was clearly waiting for me to notice her, because when I did, she gave me a subtle nod and then disappeared behind the stairs.

I frowned. I hadn't expected to see her at the party. I guess it shouldn't have been a total shock, since she was there for the party a few nights ago. She must've known someone at the company, and I made a mental note to ask her who it was later. I wasn't sure if she was trying to signal for me to come talk to her, but I felt weird introducing her to Liam. Maybe it was jealousy, or maybe it was just me being antisocial, but I didn't want the two of them to meet. Even without ever seeing them together, something about the idea put me off, like anticipating a bad chemical reaction.

After William had been enforced to endure lap dances from a team of oiled up male strippers, Liam and I found ourselves a quieter space away from the main group of the party and Grammy's non-stop catcalls.

Liam took a sip of his drink and gave me the kind of eyebrow raise and sigh that was universal shorthand for "well, that was interesting."

I nodded. "I've learned it's best if you don't stop to question anything that happened. I pretty much sectioned off a portion of my brain for dumping all the William and Grammy-related memories. I don't think about those if I can avoid it."

"Good advice. They seem fun, though. Must be nice working for a guy who isn't a hard ass."

I reached behind Liam and squeezed his ass. "Hard asses aren't so bad."

He laughed.

"But no, it's not *bad*. It's just not what I want." I felt my breath catch a little. I hadn't even told Emily about the fact that I was pursuing a business degree, or about my real dreams. I didn't know why, but of all the things I kept to myself, it felt like the most precious. Yet I could feel it rising up, like the urge to share it with Liam was a building pressure that would make me burst if I held it in for much longer.

"What do you want?" he asked.

"It's stupid, but remember how I said my parents decided they couldn't have their business guru because they never had a boy?"

He nodded slowly, and I could see understanding already seeping into his features. His inherent grasp of where my motivations came from made me fall for him even harder. It made me feel like I wasn't so silly or ridiculous for using such a trivial thing to drive me to my goal.

"Yeah," I said. "I guess I've always been about metaphorical middle fingers. What better way to make them pay for the way they raised me than to become their dream son, minus the penis, and to do it without their help? Oh, and to never give them a dime, no matter how much they beg."

Liam nodded appreciatively. "I wondered about that part. Some kids get so screwed up in the head that in your shoes, they'd still want to give money to their parents if they did make it big."

"I'm screwed up in the head, but not like that. They're currently running a car wash into the ground with their latest ill-advised loan. I don't think I'm cruel enough to ever let them go hungry or homeless, but that's as far as my mercy goes. So yeah, it's probably all a pointless fantasy, anyway. I set out to become some business badass, and here I am, years later, working as a secretary for that idiot and slowly building up crippling debt to get my Master's degree."

"Am I allowed to offer you a job?"

"No. The power fantasy is me doing something awesome and becoming the femme phenom of the business world. Not the 'sucked dick to the top' phenom."

"Technically, you haven't sucked my dick. Not that I'm keeping track or anything, but it's worth noting."

I raised an eyebrow. "I'll do it when you beg."

He laughed. "I don't remember making you beg to be eaten out. *Either time*," he added.

"That's because you're too nice and you passed up an opportunity to assert your dominance. I'm not going to make the same mistake. Beg, and I'll do it. Otherwise, no sucky sucky."

There was a challenging flicker in his eyes. "If I get you horny enough, you'll be the one begging *me*."

"Oh, I doubt it."

"I don't."

"Besides, how can you get me horny against my will? I'm pretty much immune to the usual acts of seduction. The two times we've been together, I *chose* to be seduced. There's a big difference."

He grinned wolfishly. "Now you've made a mistake. I don't know if you know this about me, but I'm competitive as hell, and you just challenged me."

"Somehow, I think I'll survive."

He took a step closer. I stood my ground, which may or may not have been a mistake, because he was close enough that I could feel the heat pouring off his skin. My mind lit up with still frames of when we'd been together. Images of my fingers pressed into his sweat-beaded skin. The way my heels looked as they wrapped around his slim, muscular waist and slid against his hard ass. The way it felt when he breathed heat into my neck during his climax, and the way the scruff on his face scratched against my chest as he kissed me like he was starving for more.

I swallowed, and it was, unfortunately, one of those cartoon swallows that made a loud clicking sound. He apparently had a talent for drawing those out of me. With considerable effort, I kept my eyes locked on his. *Don't show weakness. Don't let him see that his penis has infiltrated your mind already. Don't let him sense that your vagina, which has been mute your entire life, has spontaneously found a direct path to your thoughts and is currently trying to rewire the stubborn section of your brain so you'll just give this gorgeous man exactly what he wants.*

He put his thumb on my lower lip and studied it. Every movement was deliberate. Slow. *Careful.*

"It's a lip," I quipped, hoping to dispel some of the magic he was already working over me. "You looked confused by it," I said when his eyes flicked up to mine with dangerous intensity.

"I was just imagining how good it'd feel on my cock."

"Oh. I see you're going with the direct approach here. Can I be direct too?"

"Please."

"As much as I probably *would* enjoy it, I'm not about to get on my knees and suck you off in the middle of my boss' birthday party. I'm also too stubborn to do it now that you said you'd make me beg, so we're kind of at an impasse here."

"What do you suggest?"

"Ever hear about classical conditioning? Basically, it shows that people can be trained just like animals. You pair a stimulus with a reward or a punishment, and you can encourage or discourage the behavior."

"Interesting, professor."

I jabbed his chest with my finger and grinned. "In other words. You should ask yourself what you had to do last time you got some action? What behavior was I rewarding?"

"My memory is fuzzy. I remember falling on my ass. I remember you dragging me off the ice by my feet. Have I struck gold yet?"

"You took me to do something cool and kinda romantic."

"Kinda? Damn. I thought the ice skating thing qualified at least as 'pretty romantic.'"

"On its own, yes. But your clumsy ass falling detracted a few points."

He smirked. "Well damn. If that was my reward for a sub-par performance, what do I get if I hit it out of the park?"

"That blowjob you seem to want so badly, maybe?"

"Deal. But you still have to beg. Your boss isn't the only one with a fragile ego, you know."

"Somehow I doubt your ego is even close to fragile. So when do I get to see your romantic gesture? Tomorrow night?"

He sighed. "I wish I could. I have to do a little after hours work tomorrow, but this weekend. I promise."

I didn't let it show, but I felt giddy. Being around Liam made me feel a lot of ways I'd told myself I shouldn't feel. Excited. Happy. Girly. *Sexy.* He made me feel like I didn't have to run from all the qualities my parents had tried so hard to hammer into me, like I could finally relax and just be me for a change.

I wondered if there was still a catch lurking, though.

There was always a catch, after all. A free vacation package if you just show up to the meeting. A free iPhone if you click this advertisement. If it looked and sounded too good to be true, it probably was. And Liam looked the part. He was way out of my league, charming, nice, and even funny when he tried. For some reason, he liked me.

So where was the catch?

BEFORE I MET LIAM, I WAS PERFECTLY DISCONTENTED TO SHOW UP to work, help William avoid his responsibilities, and then deal with whatever homework or virtual classes I had to handle that night. It was boring, and it was tedious, but I was used to it.

I knew I wasn't supposed to see him today, and I was trying my damnedest to not be a lovesick thirteen-year-old who mopes around all day because she can't hold her boyfriend's hand during study hall.

I put on my normal, mildly annoyed expression and braced myself for a long day.

The office was quieter than normal. Our floor of the building was made up of the more eccentric "idea people" who helped William think of creative and groundbreaking new ways to market for Galleon's clients. In theory, it was supposed to be a bunch of creative geniuses with massive IQs. In practice, it was more like a bunch of people who didn't understand good hygiene and would go to extreme lengths to avoid actually sitting in their chairs. It was almost like sitting in a chair was some kind of social stigma. Whatever it was, men and women on our floor were always perched on the edges of desks, on flower pots, in alcoves built into the walls, or even on the floor in kindergarten-style semi-circles for reading time.

They were all ridiculous, and I had never met anyone I actually liked among them.

So when a girl I vaguely recognized and her super thick-framed glasses and *I went to an Ivy League College* face came up to my desk, I made sure to ignore her and her subtle coughs to get my attention.

"Lilith!" She finally snapped. "Some woman is here for you. Can I send her in?"

"Who is she?"

"She said her name is Claire."

"Oh. Uh, yeah, sure. Send her in."

Claire came wandering toward my desk a minute later. She was looking around the office with an interested expression, but once she spotted me, her features darkened.

"What's going on?" I asked.

"I kind of need to admit something. And I hope you're not going to hate me for it, I really do."

"No promises," I said.

She gave a half-hearted grin. "Meeting you wasn't actually an accident. The night I hid under the front desk because a guy was giving me a hard time? Well, you actually know the guy."

"Was it William?" I asked. My heart was already pounding at the thought of that idiot betraying Hailey's trust. She was the sweetest thing in the world, and if he—

"It was Liam. He was my boyfriend at the time, and he accidentally let it slip that he'd asked the girl across the hall on a date. I've always had issues with jealousy, and I... I took it too far. I had to meet you. I wanted to see what he liked about you more than me. I dug around, found out where you'd be, and I showed up."

Distantly, I could feel my heart tightening up, like it was trying to figure out if it should keep beating or just go ahead and call it quits right now.

I frowned. "So you're saying he broke up with you to ask me out?"

"No. I'm saying he was trying to get the best of both worlds and date you on the side, or turn me into the one he was dating on the side. Who knows which. I'm saying that Liam isn't the guy he wants you to think he is. You can't trust him, and I can prove it."

My head was spinning a little and I felt lightheaded, but more than anything, a growing urge to punch Liam in the penis was rising up in me. No, a penis punch would be too good for him if what she was saying was true. I'd empty a soda can, fill it with milk—because there's nothing more disturbing than taking a sip of a drink and being wrong about what you're drinking—trick him into drinking it, and *then* punch him in the penis.

On the other hand, I'd only known Claire a few days. I had no real reason to trust her over Liam, who I admittedly also hadn't known Liam for a long time-outside the fact that he has a small freckle on the base of his impressive penis, or that he is ticklish right under his butt cheek.

"You have proof?" I asked. My voice was strained as I tried to keep the emotion I felt inside from touching my words.

"He's going on a date with someone else. Tonight. I'm guessing he wasn't available to do anything with you this evening, am I right?"

My nostrils flared. "That's right. But it doesn't prove anything. He said he had something work related."

"What about the fact that he's still been seeing me this whole time? Does that prove anything?"

I sucked in a deep breath and let it out slowly. I couldn't make sense of everything fast enough, and I had to keep fighting my natural instinct to trust Liam above all else. "According to you, maybe. That's not proof. Besides, I'm supposed to believe you stayed with him even though you knew he was seeing me? Is that what I'm supposed to believe?" I hated how desperate I sounded to prove her wrong—how desperate I was to believe Liam was the man I thought he was and not the monster she was claiming.

"I never said I was a strong person, or smart," Claire said. "So you can believe what you want, but I thought I owed it to you to tell you the truth. And if you decide you want to see for yourself, he's going to be at *Cochina La'Fleur* tonight with his date. Seven-thirty reservation for two in the private patio seating in the back."

"You can leave now," I said tightly.

She gave me a sympathetic look. "I was pissed when I first found out, too. Sorry I lied to you, for whatever that's worth."

She walked away, and I buzzed William's office. He burst out of his door with a crazed look in his eyes literally five seconds later.

"You buzzed?" he asked with a mad grin.

He'd given me the power to buzz his office nearly a year ago, and I still remember how excited he'd been about it. I think he imagined I'd be buzzing him all the time to trade jokes or whatever ridiculousness went through his head. I'd stubbornly refused to use it, opting to instead wait until he inevitably left his office to wander aimlessly around the building every few minutes.

"Do you still have all that spy gear?"

"Not only do I still have it. I've upgraded since last time."

14

LIAM

Price sat across from my desk with a serious look on his face. I was due to meet with the business contact in about an hour, and he had insisted on trying to coach me up for it.

"So," he said. "What do you do if she shows doubts about the product?"

"I let the numbers do the talking. We out-perform every single financial advisor in the country over a six-month period by as much as twenty percent."

"Wrong. You empathize with her. She already knows our numbers. She's not meeting with you so you can spew out what she could read for herself. She wants to meet because she needs to feel like she trusts the people behind the numbers."

"Empathize with her? What do you want me to do, laugh and say I have my doubts too? That I always wonder which month will be the one where we fall flat on our asses and lose our investors tens of millions?"

"Uh, no. You empathize without ever taking away from our product. You compliment her for being so careful. She's a studious businesswoman. You respect that. You can't believe some people call themselves businessmen and women when they don't take the same precautions she does. *Then* you refer back to the numbers as if she has already looked at them and seen for herself that they are impressive."

"Yeah, I get it. I still don't think any of this is necessary. I mean, our product *does* speak for itself. We don't just have an edge on the competition, we swallow it up. There's literally no reason to say no."

Price sighed. "Too confident. You sound like you're trying too hard to convince her. When a salesman pushes too hard, the client gets defensive. They feel like prey and like you're the predator. You've got to make her feel like you're on her side, and you have no real stake in whether she chooses us or not. You're just a friend who is presenting her options, and the option is so clear you don't have to push her toward it."

I sighed. "Okay. Are we done?"

He crossed his arms. "Well, one more thing. She's a woman, and she's pretty. I know you've got that thing going with your neighbor, but you might want to consider flirting. I'm obviously not saying you should actually try anything. Just a little nod here, a little slightly-too-lingering look at her cleavage, a hand on the small or her back, you know, that kind of thing."

"No. Absolutely not."

Price groaned. "Come on, man. Can you at least compliment what she's wearing? It's part of the game."

"I'm already pissed enough that I had to pass up on a night with Lilith to do *your job* in the first place. I finally found a girl I like, and I'm not going to fuck it up over a few dollars."

"If this woman is who she says she is, it's more than a few dollars. A few hundred million dollars, maybe."

"What do you mean if she's who she says she is?"

Price winced. "I mean, it's not completely unheard of for a liaison to be unlisted anywhere online in connection to the company, or for her to not offer to send any kind of credentials."

"*What?*"

"I'm just saying I kind of have her word to go on, but I didn't want to insult her or them by digging and questioning whether she was legit. But why would someone lie? It's not like we're giving them money. We're trying to get them to link up thousands of accounts to use our system. There's nothing in this for a scammer, so..."

"You didn't ask for credentials?"

"I've never had to ask before. Like I said though, it's not anything you should worry about. The worst case scenario is she's some kind of psycho who gets off on pretending to be a liaison for a high-powered super corporation. I've heard about people being afraid of pickles, but I've never heard of *that* particular psychological disorder. I think we're safe."

"If this backfires somehow, I'm holding you responsible. You know that, right?"

"Backfires? What's the worst that can happen? You get to eat a fancy-ass dinner and you spend two hours talking to a psycho? Big deal. The flip side is huge. Just think about the money we could make."

"Yeah, because we need more of that."

Price pulled his head back and frowned. "Woah. Where's that coming from? What happened to the guy I knew? The one who started all of this? The one who always pushed for more and for better, even if there was no reason to?"

"When I need to use you as a therapist, I'll let you know. How does that sound?"

He gave me a tight smile. "Shit, man. I don't care if it's me. But you should at least have someone to talk to. Just saying I'm here if you need me. No homo."

I shook my head and grinned. "Really? No homo? What is this, middle school? Besides, I'm pretty sure you can't say something like that anymore. People will think you're anti-gay."

"You don't have to *be* gay to be pro-gay rights, dude. Do you think before you talk?"

I sighed. "You know what I mean."

"I just thought I saw a little twinkle in your eye. I didn't want it to get weird."

"You didn't see a twinkle in my eye. Maybe you just saw how badly I wished you came with a mute button."

"That was rude."

"I do appreciate it though. If I ever thought I needed someone to talk to, I guess I'd talk to you. *No homo*," I added with a grin.

"No homo," he agreed. "Not that there's anything wrong with that?"

I grinned. "So you're saying *some* homo, then?"

Price chuckled. "Stop trying to distract me. I was trying to figure out if I could count on you to nail this liaison business?"

"I'll assume your poor choice of words was accidental. But yes, I'll get it done, assuming this woman is even who she says she is."

THE RESTAURANT WAS BUSY, BUT WE WERE USHERED THROUGH THE quietly buzzing dining room, through a section of the kitchens, and out to a third-floor patio. A single, candle-lit table and two chairs, and a heating lamp were the only pieces of furniture on the patio. I inwardly groaned in frustration at having let Price make the reservations. He had insisted, and now I knew why.

I let the woman sit down before I took my seat across from her, and it was only then that I took my first real look at her. She had platinum-blonde hair, lips so suspiciously full that I wondered if she'd had surgical assistance, and an upturned nose. She looked like some of the women I'd wasted my time with years ago—the type who showed up when enough zeroes appeared in your bank account. It was as mysterious to me as the appearance of flies around a trash can in an otherwise clean house. I could only figure it was the same mystery of science at play.

I nodded to her and gave a tight smile as the waiter filled our waters and described the featured wine selections for the night. I started to wave him off, but she touched his arm and ordered a bottle for the table. She had a European accent I couldn't place. It was somewhere between French and Italian, I thought.

The heating lamp wasn't doing much to fight against the chill in the air, so I didn't remove my coat. The woman across from me apparently felt otherwise, and when she pulled off her jacket, I felt like I had to look a few feet over her head to avoid the excessive amounts of cleavage she was displaying.

"I'm Liam, by the way," I said to the skyscraper above her head.

"Floria," she purred. "I'm not sure how much your partner told you, but I'm very interested in you and your business."

"Yes, I was told you specifically wanted to meet with me. I can assure you, though, Price is much better suited to explain our product and what it can do for you. I'm essentially just the one who has my nose buried in the stock market."

"It looks like you also find time to exercise as well. Quite vigorously, I imagine."

I clenched my teeth. Warning alarms were already sounding in my head. I may not have had Price's job, but I knew enough about schmoozing potential clients to know where the line was supposed to be drawn between professional and casual. She was already testing the boundaries.

"So what exactly do you do for your company?"

"Merrick was my great-grandfather's company." Her tone was dismissive, and she was speaking quickly, like she was building toward changing the subject as quickly as she could. "I'll be honest with you, Mr. Hightower. They mostly send me for face-to-face meetings because we've found potential business partners are more generous once they've met me. *Face-to-face*," she added as she rested her chin on the back of her hand.

I had to fight the urge to sigh with exasperation. Whatever

this was. *Whoever* she was. I wasn't buying it. I had to at least get some kind of confirmation before I called this charade off, because I knew Price would never let it go if I didn't give him some conclusive reason I'd told this woman to get lost.

I had a bad feeling it was going to be a long, frustrating night, and I couldn't stop my mind from wandering to Lilith—to wishing I was sitting across from her instead of wasting my time with this joke of a business deal.

15

LILITH

The night vision goggles had a few toggle switches that let me adjust how sensitive to heat they were. William had rented me a hotel room with a perfect view of the patio behind *Cochina La'Fleur*. Unfortunately, the windows didn't open, but I had the goggles pressed against the glass as I frowned down at the patio a few floors below me. From this distance, Liam and the woman were about the size of my thumb, but I could at least kind of see what was going on.

Liam looked like an orange and red blob, with his face being the darkest red. The woman across from him was a lighter shade of yellow, probably because the idiot had taken her jacket off to reveal a giant, hot pair of boobs—and I meant hot in the objective sense, because they were dark red orbs on her otherwise yellow-tinged body through the goggles. It was like she had some kind of super-hoe power of directing her blood flow to her boobs to engorge them for maximum *steal-yo-man* effect.

"Seeing anything cool?" William asked. He was crouched beside me. A few feet behind *him,* Hailey waited with her arms crossed and a look on her face that said she was still trying to figure out why she had married a man-child. At the same time, she couldn't seem to look at him without a glint of adoration, like she was also trying to figure out why she also couldn't help being so deeply in love with said man-child.

"I see my sort-of-boyfriend sitting across from two giant boobs attached to a woman. So, no, it doesn't seem cool to me."

"You're saying she's stacked?"

"William," groaned Hailey. "Can you refrain from talking about another woman's breasts while I'm in the room, at least?"

"It's not for my own benefit, Hailey. It's because I'm trying to put together a mental case on this whole situation. We've got the boyfriend and the mysterious date. The mysterious ex who claims to also be a girlfriend. The way this mysterious date of his looks is critical. We need to know if she's the crafty type, or just someone who is as clueless as Lilith was."

"I wasn't *clueless*. I'm still not even sure I believe any of this, for the record."

"Right," William said. "You didn't believe it so hard you practically begged me to set up this sting operation."

I set down the goggles to glare at him. "Begged you? I just asked for the goggles. You were the one who was bursting out of your boots with how bad you wanted to know what was going on."

Hailey groaned. "You said you only agreed to do all this because you'd never seen Lilith cry before. You said it was moving, and if I'd been there, I definitely would've cried."

William made an *ehh* kind of noise and hopped up to his feet. "Let's not get bogged down by details, people. We've got something more important to focus on here. Lilith's boyfriend has a case of wandering penis, and we need to find if the snake is going to find a new hole tonight."

"William," Hailey hissed. "That's her sort-of-boyfriend you're talking about. Also, you lied to drag me into this. That means I get to pick where we're having dinner tonight. That was the deal."

He sighed. "Come on. It was a *white* lie. I know what you're going to pick, and I can't do sushi again. Haven't you seen those statistics about how likely you are to get worms? Or have you seen the videos of tuna coming in off the dock just teeming with worms under their skin."

"Then you'd better chew thoroughly," Hailey said. "Because it's going to be sushi."

The two of them began arguing about where they were going to get dinner, and I re-focused on the balcony while trying to ignore them.

The waiter brought a bottle of wine to the table and poured both of them a glass. *Some business meeting.* The woman pressed her hand to her chest and tossed her head back to laugh loudly at something, and I couldn't quite make out Liam's face to see if he was smiling too.

I was gritting my teeth. Night-vision goggles weren't really helping me, here. The listening device would have been good, but the windows made it so the only thing I could hear was a hundred echoes of sound bouncing off windows throughout the building I was in.

I felt guilty for doing this, but I also thought any sane woman would at least have considered trying to investigate everything Claire said. Admittedly, most sane women probably would've settled for finding a spot on the street outside the restaurant to wait instead of the elaborate operation I'd been sucked into.

I was about to get up and go down when I saw the woman deliberately tug her dress down, revealing even more of those ridiculous boobs. Liam seemed to stiffen in his seat, and then he set his napkin down, stood, and started walking back inside the restaurant. The woman stood up, too, and followed him inside.

My stomach sank. Was that all it took? A little bonus boob and dinner was abandoned because he just couldn't wait to screw her?

"Mission's off," I said. My voice sounded dry and dead.

"What?" asked William, who had moved on from arguing

about tuna worms to how sushi was technically like throwing rice in a salad, if you really thought about it. "What happened?"

"She practically flashed him, he got up, and they both went into the restaurant. I'm just wondering if they'll make it back to a bed or if they're going to go at it in the bathroom."

"Wait," Hailey said. "Who got up first? Him?"

"Yeah, why?"

"What if he got pissed off. Maybe it *was* a business meeting and she crossed the line. He could've been walking out on her. She might have gone after him to change his mind."

I thought about that, and admittedly liked the sound of it. It helped un-sink my stomach, at least a little. "Maybe..."

"Go to him," William whispered.

I frowned up at him. "What if I 'go to him' and he's balls deep in that woman?"

"That would be an unexpected development." William rubbed his chin, deep in thought. "I think you would, at that point, tell him you had just come to let him know you caught gonorrhea from him, and he was a dirty bastard."

I nodded. "That's actually a good idea."

"Woah. You have gonorrhea? I meant as a joke."

I sighed and handed him his goggles back. "Sorry, Hailey. I've got to leave you alone with him now. By the way, he's right about the tuna worms, though, as much as I hate to admit it. I've seen the videos. He sent them out to everyone in the office a few months ago."

Hailey pursed her lips in disappointment. "The last thing William needs is somebody telling him he's right. What have you done?"

I grinned. "Somehow, I have a feeling you can figure out how to handle him."

I walked out and the grin melted from my face in seconds. I wanted to believe the good version of the story. He'd been telling me the truth, after all. It was a business meeting. The woman turned out to be a creep. He left. End of story.

I was too emotionally invested to be satisfied, though. A jealous voice in my head kept whispering all the horrible things that could be happening right now—the horrible things that had *already happened*. If Claire had been telling the truth, this wasn't even the first time he'd gone behind my back. It would've constantly been happening since we first met, and to him, I'd be nothing but a plaything to manipulate and use until he got bored.

On the other hand, I still couldn't shake the memory of what he'd told me. His step-sister was psychotic. She had claimed she'd ruin things between us, but I couldn't even begin to figure out how she could've been involved in all of this. She would've had to put Claire and this woman up to the deception, and while I didn't know the woman, it seemed like a serious stretch to think someone would go to such lengths.

There was no use agonizing over it, I figured. I wasn't going to do any more guesswork. I'd do what I should've done as soon as Claire told me her story. I was going to find Liam and confront him. I just hoped he would be fully clothed and alone when I caught up with him.

WHEN I GOT TO THE STREET BELOW, I SPOTTED LIAM WAITING ON the curb, trying to hail a cab. I stopped dead in my tracks, deciding I needed to see where he was going for myself instead of trusting that he would tell me the truth. I nearly got knocked to the ground when the man behind me bumped into my back.

"Learn to walk, dickweed!" I barked.

The man turned a surprised eye toward me, but kept walking.

I breathed out my annoyance, and then I hid behind an outcropping in the building while I watched after Liam. He was still trying to hail a cab.

I'd hardly ever used a cab in my life, especially once Uber

came about, but I made a snap decision to follow him. Whether I wanted to believe it or not, I had to accept the fact that Claire could have been telling the truth. So far, I hadn't so much as caught a hint of Liam lying to me past his hidden identity, which he had pretty readily confessed to. That meant he either wasn't lying, or he was a good liar. Following him might be my only chance to catch him in the act, even if I did feel guilty about it.

A cab pulled up for me almost immediately, and when I glanced toward Liam, I saw he was getting in one as well.

The cab driver was a woman in her twenties with facial piercings and bright purple hair done up in pigtails. She turned to face me with a surprisingly inviting smile.

"Hey, hey!" She said.

"This is going to sound super cliché, but I need you to follow that cab." I leaned forward and pointed to Liam's cab in her rearview mirror.

Her eyes followed my finger and narrowed. I thought she was about to laugh at me or tell me to get out, but instead, she balled her hand into a small fist and nodded her head slowly.

"Hell. Yes. I've literally been waiting for someone to ask me to do this since I started this job."

I sat back and looked a little wearily at her. She looked *too* excited, and I hoped she understood I wasn't expecting a Hollywood car chase.

Liam's cab pulled past, and the woman gunned the gas, cutting off a car and getting directly behind Liam's cab.

"We should probably not follow directly behind him, just in case," I advised.

"Shit," she hissed. She yanked the wheel to the left, cutting across incoming traffic to jam her cab crookedly between two parked cars, then swerved back across traffic, cutting off more cars. We were now a few cars behind Liam, and she gave me a triumphant thumbs up while a storm of honking horns rang out behind us.

"That was one way to do it," I said quietly.

She followed somewhat uneventfully for the rest of the trip, keeping a few cars between us and thankfully avoiding more dramatic driving maneuvers, for the most part.

I stuck my hand out and made sure my back was to Liam. I was only a few dozen yards up the street from him, but it was busy enough that I didn't think there was a significant chance of being spotted.

16

LIAM

I sat in the back of the cab and seethed. The "liaison" had my sister written all over her. I tried calling Lilith for the sixth time since storming out of the restaurant, but got her voicemail again.

I had a sinking feeling that my sister wouldn't go through the trouble of hiring an actress and duping Price into thinking she was legit just for laughs. She had promised to screw things up between Lilith and me, giving me no doubt she would've made sure Lilith saw some angle of the dinner and gotten the wrong idea. I thought back to the way the woman had flashed her cleavage so blatantly and tried so hard to look flirtatious. So hard that you could've spotted it from blocks away.

I wanted to break something just thinking about how I'd walked right into Celia's plan. But how would she have made sure Lilith could see? Was I just being paranoid?

I tried calling Lilith again and nearly squeezed the life out of my phone when she didn't answer. I nearly told the driver to turn around and take me back to my apartment because Lilith might be home, but I knew in my gut that she wasn't. Whatever Celia had arranged, Lilith wouldn't just be sitting at home, watching TV.

Celia, on the other hand, would be waiting with a gloating smile on her face. She was probably sitting just by the front door so she could see the look on my face as quick as humanly possible. I had to find out what she had told Lilith so I'd know where to start when it came time to unravel the lies. I had an idea, too. It was a messy idea, and it was messy enough that I hadn't wanted to resort to it yet. I pulled out my phone and decided there was no mess too big now, no line too firm to cross.

I called Celia's husband and waited for him to pick up.

I GOT OUT OF THE CAB AND JOGGED TO THE FRONT DOOR OF CELIA'S house. I knocked hard and waited. I wasn't surprised when the door opened only a couple of seconds later to reveal my sister, who was wearing a ridiculously elaborate white dress with black gemstone jewelry to match her hair.

She looked up at me through lazy, triumphant eyes and smiled. "Brother."

"Step-brother," I corrected. "What the fuck did you do?"

"You mean this evening? I had a hair appointment and then I went to the—"

"You know what I'm asking. What. Did. You. Do?"

She blew out a puff of air through her nose, letting some of the evil in her heart touch her features for once. "I did exactly what I said I'd do. I did what I'll *continue* to do if you don't give me what I want."

"What you want. Refresh my memory on that."

"You know exactly what I want. If you're perverted enough to need to hear it out loud, then I'll be happy to oblige. I want to *fuck* you. Not because I love you. Not because I want a relationship with you. I want it because you told me no, and nobody tells me no."

I pursed my lips and nodded. "What happens when your husband finds out?"

"It doesn't matter, because he won't. I've been outsmarting you without any trouble this whole time, and you're considerably more capable than poor Walter. He'll stay the dark for as long as I want him to."

I grinned, feeling a surge of triumph. I raised my voice and projected it into the house. "Did you hear enough, Walter, or do you still want more proof?"

I waited for the color to drain from Celia's face, but she only watched me with that same, self-satisfied smile.

"Walter?" I called.

"Your mistake was calling him too early. You gave me a few minutes to convince him my poor, delicate heart would be broken if he really believed the lies you were telling him."

She saw the look on my face and laughed. "You don't really think I let him receive calls without listening in, do you? Anyway, he's not going to be coming to eavesdrop on our conversation. He's still lying in bed, and he's happy. He doesn't *want* to believe anything bad about me, you know. He wants me to be his perfect little angel, and he'll keep turning a blind eye to any hints or whispers that I'm not because he'd rather live in the illusion. So you might as well give up your silly attempts to *expose* me to him now."

Both our heads turned when another car pulled up in the driveway. I couldn't see the driver past the headlights, but when the door opened, there was no mistaking Lilith as she stepped out slowly.

"Oh," Celia tried to step back in the house and close the door.

On instinct, I took hold of her wrist firmly enough to let her know she wasn't slipping away. I didn't know why, but I knew she wanted to bolt at the sight of Lilith, and that was reason enough.

"Lilith," I said over my shoulder. "Have you ever met my sister?"

Lilith came closer. She was walking slowly and the car behind her was still idling. I saw her eyes darting around, trying to take everything in at once. I could practically hear the hum of her brain piecing everything together.

"Your sister," she said.

"It's what he does," Celia said in a somewhat strange tone. She almost sounded like someone else. Less evil, at the least. "He comes up with insane lies when he gets caught. Don't believe a word he says."

17

LILITH

I stared in disbelief as Liam held Claire by the wrist. Every insecure molecule of my brain was trying to convince me to believe *her*. To believe everything, because what other explanation could there be for a man like Liam being interested in me?

But that was dumb. Idiotic, even. Liam had already given me something he couldn't take away, even if Claire had told the truth all along about him. He let me believe I was worth caring about. Whether he actually cared or not didn't matter. I still had that belief tucked away deep in my chest, and it wasn't the kind of gift he could take back.

Yet I didn't think he wanted to. I looked at Claire and her desperate eyes, at the way she was *still* trying to tug free from him. Why would she try to duck inside when she saw me if she was telling the truth? Wouldn't this moment be a triumph for her? Physical proof that Liam was a jerk and he'd come to see his ex at her doorstep?

"So you were Liam's sister the whole time," I said, shaking my head at my own idiocy. I wasn't sure how I let the woman dupe me so thoroughly, and how I'd almost fallen for the biggest dupe of all. I spied on Liam and let my mind go to the darkest corners of possibility, believing he was possible of so many horrible things. Still, I couldn't imagine what she thought would happen. I'd watch them walk off together and just cut ties with him? Maybe she thought seeing the "date" would shake my trust in him enough that he'd never have a chance of winning me back.

"Wait, the whole time?" Liam looked between us, then back at her. "How long have you known Lilith? Who does she think you are?"

Claire—no, *Celia*. I remembered the name from one of the first long conversations I'd had with Liam. *Celia* jerked her arm free from Liam. I thought she was about to give some sort of evil villain speech, or maybe pull a mask off and say she'd have gotten away with it if it wasn't for those meddling kids and that dog, but instead, she slammed the door on both of us without another word.

The last fleeting image I had was of her in the doorway with a twisted, mean expression on her face—an expression mean enough to match the imposing widow's peak I had initially thought was so distinctive.

Liam looked down at his hand where he'd been touching her wrist and wiped it on his pants absentmindedly. "If you think she's nice, wait till you meet my parents."

I laughed, even though I didn't feel like laughing, not entirely. "Considering I don't see Miss Megaboob around, I'm going to assume you weren't bolting out of your chair back at the restaurant to get some action in a bathroom." I winced as soon as I finished speaking. I'd just admitted to spying on him, and the grin he wore told me he hadn't missed the fact.

"Bird watching again?" he asked.

I sighed. "Boob watching, more accurately. Those things were giving off so much heat it was hard to see much else."

Liam laughed. "It's okay. Celia has a lifetime of practice at twisting facts around and manipulating people. And I forgive you for spying on me."

"I didn't ask to be forgiven. But I appreciate it," I added with a sigh. I looked toward Celia's house and scowled. "Also, we're going to bring that bitch down."

"When I found out about the cameras, I wanted nothing more than to watch her life come crashing down around her. I still do. I guess the difference now is if I had to choose between you and revenge, I'd choose you."

"Good thing you don't have to pick one. Let's put it this way. If I had a penis, I would have a revenge boner right now."

Liam choked out a laugh. "I'm... pretty sure I've never heard of that before."

"It's when you get a boner because—"

He held up a hand, his grin widening. "The phrase is self-explanatory. I just meant I don't know if penises work that way."

"Mine would," I said quietly, never taking my eyes from Celia's house. "It would be throbbing right now and pointed straight toward that evil, cold bitch."

"I'm not sure if I'm supposed to be aroused by that, but I'm sorry, I'm not."

I shifted my eyes to him. "This isn't about arousal, Liam. It's about revenge."

"You know, I came here ready to tear her house down with my bare hands if I had to, and now you're making *me* feel like the rational one."

"I never told you what happened to the kids who bullied me in school."

"You never told me you were bullied."

"Yeah, well, I was. It was how I met my best friend, Emily. She stepped in and defended me, which meant all kinds of grief between her snooty friends. But I got every single one of them back. All the girls who picked on me. Every last one of them paid."

Liam looked at me very seriously, his face lit by the still-idling cab a dozen yards away in Celia's driveway. "Did you... *hurt them?*"

"Physically, no. Emotionally, yes. I replaced one girl's moisturizer with mayonnaise and watched as she slathered her legs and hands in mayo during first-period English. I convinced another one she was pen pals with Aaron Carter—he was big at the time —and that he was in love with her, and once she professed her own love, he stopped writing. I paid for a wake-up call service on the last bully at random times during the school day every day until she eventually got her phone confiscated. That was all phase one, and I had two more phases planned if they didn't leave me alone afterwards, but I never had to take it that far. With your step-sister, I think we need to jump straight to phase three."

He looked seriously concerned by now. "Phase three isn't murder, is it?"

"Do you really think I'm capable of murder?"

"Do you really want me to answer that?"

"I don't have a concrete plan yet for what we're going to do, but it's going to teach her to fuck off, once and for all. I know that much."

LIAM AND I TOOK MY CAB BACK INTO THE CITY AND STOPPED AT A late-night cafe. He ordered us some frozen yogurt and coffee. His was some kind of cookie dough and brownie monstrosity, while mine was a more sensible chocolate and oreo concoction.

For all my talk of revenge boners, it felt amazing just to sit and eat dessert with him. Nearly losing him made me appreciate him even more than I already had, and I could already feel a little bit of what he meant about the thirst for revenge being hard to focus on. Then again, I still wasn't going to let that bitch get away with what she did.

"I never understood people who eat cookie dough," I said as I swallowed a mouthful of my treat.

He furrowed his eyebrows. "What do you mean? It's a pretty common thing. It tastes amazing."

"Name me any other food where people purposefully order it before it's finished being cooked."

"It's different."

"I'm pretty sure there's raw egg in cookie dough. You're probably going to spend all night on the toilet after that, assuming you don't drop dead before then."

"I'm pretty sure the business wouldn't survive with a topping that was poisoning or killing people on their menu. Besides, my digestive system is impenetrable. I could eat three hamburgers and fries for breakfast without so much as a cramp. I think I'll survive."

"Next you're going to tell me your poop is solid gold and it doesn't smell."

"Wait, that's not normal?" he asked.

I rolled my eyes. "Just eat your poison and let me think about how I'm going to get revenge on your sister."

He was quiet for a while, and when he finally spoke, there was a more serious note in his voice. "I feel like I'm supposed to apologize for all of this, but I'm also worried if I apologize, it's going to seem like I did something to make this all happen."

"You can always apologize for not snuffing your sister out when you still had the chance. Accidentally let her get lost in the woods on a family trip, that sort of thing."

"You're horrible. But for some reason, I still like you."

"You *like* me, huh?"

He flashed something between a smile and a frown. "You're just figuring this out?"

"No. I just like hearing you say it."

"Lilith. We don't have to even think about my sister. She did her worst already. She tried to screw things up with us, and she failed. Move in with me. Come live in my real apartment. You can even bring your weird cat."

"Roosevelt isn't weird, but I don't think that's a good idea. Not yet. You said she has done her worst, but I don't think she has.

Something tells me you never had to deal with bullies, but I have. They don't usually give up unless you punch back. Hunkering down and hoping it goes away usually makes it worse. Think about it. What have you done since your sister started waging this war against you? Changed your identity? Tried to lay low? You need to grow a pair and kick her back where it hurts. Punch first before she can punch harder."

"Hey," he said. "The choices I made weren't because I was afraid. I didn't want to waste my time with her and her games. I thought the fastest way to get it all over with would be to ignore it. But don't think for a second that I'm not willing to do something. I just don't think we have to anymore. She has to see that she lost. Didn't you see the way she looked at you?"

"Yeah, like I was a new wrinkle in an ongoing plan. She's not done, trust me."

"So what are you thinking? How do we get her to stop?"

"You said she's married, right?"

He nodded.

"That's our answer. Either she's actually in love with the man, or she's sticking with him for the money. One way or another, she wants it to stay the way it is. So we hit her where it hurts. We find a way to expose her."

"Is it bad that I'm more interested in getting *you* exposed?"

"Yes," I said, but I couldn't completely stop myself from smiling. "You're bad. And I've reconsidered. I'll stay in your apartment. Temporarily. But Roosevelt needs his own space. That's my condition."

"He can have his own room."

"Ugh. I forgot how disgustingly rich you are."

As it turned out, disgustingly rich was an understatement.

Liam's apartment was a hollowed out section of a skyscraper downtown. We entered through a luxury hotel lobby, rode up sixty floors, and exited into his "penthouse suite." I'd come to think of penthouses as being the top-most floor of a building, but his was more like the top four floors combined into one massive living space.

"How does this even work?" I asked. We stepped out of the elevator and I had to do a slow, rotating spin to take everything in. Sweeping views of downtown New York in every direction, with only a handful of buildings tall enough to stand above us. Deep, gold-veined marble floors stretched in every direction, but were made less cold and severe by splashes of plush, white and gray fabrics draped over modern furniture or splayed out as rugs. "Is this like a hotel room you rent indefinitely?"

"Not exactly. The original owner of the hotel sold the top floors to his billionaire friend forty years back. When his friend moved, it became available for purchase, and I snagged it. But I do still get room service if I want, so there's that."

I paused beside his coffee table, where what looked like a solid bar of gold the size of my hand was simply sitting in plain view. I tried to pick it up, but it was either glued in place or far heavier than it looked.

"What's with this?" I asked, grunting with the effort of picking it up. I was about to give up and assume it was stuck in place when I finally got my fingers under the lip and pried it up into the air. It felt like it weighed five pounds, even though it was the size of a deck of cards.

"Gold," he said.

I scrunched up my face at him. "Seriously? Was there a point where you got so much money that you were just like, 'oh, I know what the perfect decoration for this table would be. *Solid gold*'?"

"Actually, no," he said, gently taking it from my hand and studying the metal. "I got it when I was feeling a little dramatic. I thought it was a good symbol, I guess."

"A symbol for what? How loaded you are?"

"No." He met my eyes and then looked away, flashing a rare

moment of vulnerability. "Forget it." He lobbed the gold to his couch like it was a useless paperweight and not worth more than most people's houses.

"I don't want to forget it. You were about to give me some backstory. I could feel it. I need to know, especially now that you're trying to get out of telling me. Think about it. You practically know everything about me. But what do I really know about you?"

"You know plenty."

"I know your step-sister has a lady boner for you and I know you're rich. That's about it."

"I'm hurt. What about my charming personality?"

"Okay. I know you aren't the biggest ass I've ever met."

He considered my words, then nodded with a purse of his lips. "I'll take it."

"You will. *And* you're going to tell me the story on that." I emphasized my point by jabbing my finger at the gold bar.

Liam sank down onto the couch and palmed the metal again, looking at it while he spoke. "It's really not a big deal. I just... I was thinking about where I was. *In life*," he said a little quietly, like it was physically painful for him to be talking this deeply about his feelings. "I decided I'd been wasting my life. All I cared about was work, making more money, finding more success. I was tired of letting good things go by."

"I'm not trying to be rude here, but I don't get how any of this has to do with you having a solid gold bar on your coffee table."

"Well, I was a little drunk. And I bought it a few days ago."

"Oh. The way you were talking, I thought this was some big life crisis you'd had a few years ago. You're talking about just a few days ago?"

"Yeah. When I met you. Drunken me thought it made perfect sense. I could leave behind the old me and this would be my little trophy to remember what good all the money got me." He hefted the gold bar and chuckled. "I told you it was dumb."

"Not dumb. Maybe a little melodramatic. But I get it. You're using it like a paperweight, so drunken Liam was saying money wasn't really good for much? *While not drunken Liam lives in a massive, multi-million dollar penthouse?*"

He bit his lip. "I'll give you that one. But let me have my brooding symbolism, won't you?"

"You know," I said suddenly, holding up my finger. "I think we need to clear the air on where we stand, because if we're talking high school rules here, oral sex and well... *penis sex* all kind of implies a relationship. You don't have to do the formal asking out of... the other person, but I also feel like I don't even know if I'm allowed to call you my boyfriend."

He was grinning at me with raised eyebrows as he stood and took my hands. "Lilith... Will you be my girlfriend?"

"Yes," I said. "But only if you let me hold that gold bar again. I felt like an evil super villain with it in my hands."

"I could get you some more gold. Maybe gold coins? We could fill a kiddie pool with them and you could swim around in it. If it's what my girlfriend wants, that is."

"Right now, what your girlfriend really wants is to satisfy this revenge boner I have for your sister. If we don't take care of it soon, I'm going to get the revenge equivalent of blue balls. *Red balls?*"

"How about the one where you don't have balls. Or a raging erection. I think I like your parts as they are."

"You *think*?" I asked, throwing my shoulders back and ramming him with my boobs.

He stumbled back, but the smile he wore was the dangerous kind, not the humorous kind. His hand was already snaking around behind my back, searching for a shortcut into my dress and finding the zipper at the back. "My memory is fuzzy lately. But you could always refresh it."

"What about all the windows up here? I don't want some

random dude on the street asking me about the mole on my right butt cheek tomorrow.

"There's a mole on your right butt cheek?" Liam asked.

"Possibly. I could show you if you forget about your stupid thing where you thought I'd get on my knees and beg to give you a blowjob."

"I *had* forgotten about that," he said, slapping his forehead with his palm. "How nice of you to remind me. No. I think I'll still take my begging on the knees, *and* that mole on your ass. Maybe I'll bite it."

"Definitely not begging," I said.

"So you'll get on your knees for me?"

"No." I crossed my arms and gave him my best glare. "Why are you looking at me like that? I don't like that look..."

He put a hand on my back, and in a blurring series of movement, I felt a quick jolt of pressure at the back of my knees, bending them involuntarily forward. Instead of my knees banging to the floor, he caught my shoulders and sat me gently down.

Liam cleared his throat. "Glad you changed your mind."

"What the hell was that? Kung fu?"

"Judo, actually."

"Okay. Pause. You know Judo?"

"A man has to have a hobby."

"I'll make you a new deal. If you teach me how to do that, I'll do anything you want."

His eyebrows shot up.

18

LIAM

I usually left schmoozing potential clients at snooty parties to Price, but I wasn't about to pass the opportunity to distract Lilith from her quest to satisfy her "revenge boner" against Celia. I almost hated to admit it, but I was having trouble summoning up the desire to focus on Celia in any capacity. It finally felt like nothing was standing between Lilith and I. Deep down, I knew Lilith was probably right about Celia; my step-sister wasn't going to accept that she had lost without a last-ditch effort to sabotage. And yet, to me, Celia felt like an unimportant speed bump standing between Lilith and I. I would've been happy to slow down, roll over her, and leave her in the rearview.

Lilith, on the other hand, wanted to get out of the car with a sledgehammer and some dynamite to blow the speed bump clear out of the pavement. But that was her style, and it was part of her charm. She was an odd balance of girliness and commando. Her childhood had done a real number on her, and since we'd met, I felt like I was watching her break away from her past moment by moment. I enjoyed it, and I was excited to see how far she could really take her transformation.

She stood beside me in a sleek green dress that glimmered

like fish scales. It had a deep, open back that I kept feeling my eyes wander to. I drank in the subtle crease of muscle traveling down her spine and fading away to the soft skin above her ass, knowing that I could effortlessly slide my hand under the fabric to steal a handful if I wanted.

I controlled myself. I knew I could have her again soon. It had been nearly a week since our little judo lesson, which had led to a blowjob lesson. Watching her admit it was her first time when her fingers were wrapped around me and her lips were inches from the head of my cock might have been the sexiest thing I'd ever seen. To be honest, I couldn't have known it was her first time, but I may have been guilty of dragging it out by giving her new techniques to try. She was a fast learner, and as it turned out, she was eager to get in practice as often as she could.

One of my goals was to make sure that box of her sex toys she'd brought along with her stuff when she "temporarily" moved in with me stayed taped shut. I didn't want to share her, not even with a sex toy. I was also taking quiet pleasure in the fact that she kept bringing more "temporary" boxes over every day, and those boxes had a tendency to end up opened and unpacked.

Price, for once, was fully buttoned up in a tux.

I reached out and plucked at his collar. "Did your grandma dress you today?" I asked

"Believe it or not," he said, flicking my hand away like I was a fly. "I am actually good at my job, and I did my research. There's a big fish here today, and sloppy dressers are one of his pet peeves. *So.*"

"So you finally admit your style is sloppy and not fashionable?"

"No. I just know that somebody so close-minded wouldn't appreciate my style anyway." Price looked to Lilith, who had wandered toward a table full of food and drinks. "How's it going with her, by the way?"

"Fine," I said.

"Come on. I've caught you smiling at least ten times in the last week. I even heard you whistling in your office once. Admit it. It's more than fine."

I shrugged. "I think I love her."

Price did a double take, bulging his eyes at me. "Love?"

"She's all I think about. I don't even care about getting back at Celia anymore."

Price shook his head. "Of course she's all you're thinking about. It's like Romeo and Juliet, man. Why do you think all the tragic romances are about people who barely spent any time together? You think Romeo would've killed himself if he'd lived with Juliet long enough to realize she can't clean up her fucking socks off the bathroom floor? Or that she gets crazy gassy after she eats Mexican? Come on. It's up here," he said, tapping my head. "It's biology playing tricks on you. All your body wants is for you to put a baby in her, pass on your genes, and then boom. The magic chemicals turn off and you'll realize love is just an illusion."

"*Or*," I said. "You're a cynical dick and you don't know anything about love because you've never been in a serious relationship."

"Define serious."

"Something that lasts more than a month."

He looked like he was about to say I was wrong, and then frowned. "You don't need first-hand experience to see it, Liam. Think about it. What happens when you run out of stuff to talk about, or when the sex isn't as fun anymore? You really want to lock yourself into one woman for the rest of your life based on a week or two of knowing her?"

"I didn't say I was going to marry her, but I *was* thinking about it."

He closed his eyes and put his fingertips to his forehead. "You're pussy sick. That's all this is. It will pass, but I need you to promise you won't tell her you 'love' her yet. Once you do that, you're going to set a dangerous chain of events into play, and I can't promise I'll be able to pull you out of it."

"I appreciate the concern, but I think I can handle myself. I know how I feel. It's as simple as that."

"Just a few seconds ago you said you *think* you love her. Now you're talking like it's certain."

"I made up my mind since then."

He let out an exasperated sigh. "Does Kade know? One of us should tell him. It's going to break the poor little guy's heart."

Kade popped into the conversation, somehow managing to surprise me, even though it wasn't usually hard to track his huge body. "I already know, Price. Liam told me when we got here. Guess that means I'm his best friend."

Price scoffed. "He only told you first because he knew you were too simple-minded to call him out for being an idiot."

"Simple-minded?" Kade asked. "Who do you think wrote the code for the 'genius' software you can never stop raving about to our clients, and—"

I wandered away to let the two of them bicker. The real reason neither of them had ever been in a serious relationship was probably that they ended up arguing with each other at almost every opportunity.

Lilith was watching something with a wide, eager expression I hadn't ever seen on her face.

"What's going on?" I asked as I moved in beside her.

"That woman. She has toilet paper stuck to her heel, and she just got done telling off a waiter for offering her wine because she's pregnant, even though she's obviously not showing. See how people are starting to notice the toilet paper but nobody's saying anything?"

I watched the woman saunter her way through the room with half-lidded, confident eyes. Behind her, an occasional head would turn. It seemed relatively uneventful, but Lilith looked enthralled. "I'm surprised nobody's telling her."

"I'm not. I see stuff like this all the time. People hardly ever say anything, unless it's a close friend. Regular people just like to watch and point it out to their friends."

I grinned. "Kind of messed up. But if you ever have toilet paper stuck to your shoe, I'll tell you right away."

"Not necessary. Getting toilet paper stuck to your shoe is a mystery I've never quite figured out. I mean, what are people doing in bathrooms where they're stepping on toilet paper? Aren't they watching where they walk in public restrooms in the first place? I've seen enough rogue turds on the ground in sketchy bathrooms that my eyes are pretty much locked on the floor."

"That's a good point."

"What?" she asked. "You're looking at me funny."

I nodded past her. "Not at you," I said quietly. "She's here."

"Oh shit." Lilith hissed.

We'd worked out the plan over the past week, and Celia's arrival was phase one. I grabbed a shrimp from the assortment of food on the nearby table and launched it at Price. It ricocheted off his forehead. His head tipped back comically, like he'd just been shot between the eyes. He looked at me with an *I'm about to murder you* scowl.

"Celia," I mouthed, jerking my head toward her.

He shushed Kade and then hurried off into the crowd. Price promised he knew a guy who could "sell a speedo to an Eskimo." We just needed this guy to sell a story to Celia, which might be harder.

He came back a few seconds later with a well-dressed man a little older than me. He was good-looking, and gave me a knowing wink as he walked toward Celia.

"You really think this is going to work?" Lilith asked me.

"Don't stare," I said. "Celia knows we're here, but if she sees us watching her too closely she's probably going to start getting suspicious."

"How long do you think it will take her to fall for this if it *does* work?"

"I don't know. But Price and I are giving this guy access to our money, so he should be able to sell the fact that he's loaded pretty easily. Celia has always been a gold digger, but she's prideful, too. If she can have her rich whale of a husband *and* have him be young and good looking, I think she'll jump at the chance. It's like a trophy to her, and she wants the best, shiniest one. So if this guy can make her think that's what he is, I think it could actually work."

"So he seduces her, convinces her to divorce her husband, and then he just drops her."

"Unless you want to call it off," I said.

She shook her head. "Think about everything she did. The camera. Miss Megaboobs. I mean, trying to get somebody to divorce their husband *is* kind of taking things up a few notches, I'll admit, but I don't want to call it off. Revenge boner, remember?"

"I remember. I feel a little bad about this. I have to be honest."

"We're not backing out, bucko." She sounded more confident now. "Think about it. If by some miracle, she actually cares about her husband, she wouldn't even think about divorcing him in the first place. This only works if the marriage was a sham to begin with."

Price joined us. "This guy is a pro. Trust me. He could sell salt to a snail."

"I thought it was speedos to Eskimos," I said.

"It's both. He's a natural. Absolutely no remorse. Honestly, the guy always strikes me as a bit of a sociopath, so I doubt this will even psychologically scar him."

"I want to ruin Celia's life, not *end* it. If this guy is dangerous, we need to call the plan off."

Price held up his palms to me. "Easy. Poor choice of words. Besides, I said a *bit* of a sociopath. I just mean most guys I bring into sales get all moral about tricking people into buying something they shouldn't have. He just wants the sale. Doesn't care if it's good or bad for the client. Trust me, he's the man for this job."

"What did you say his name was?"

"Florian."

Lilith choked back a laugh.

"What?" Price asked.

"He doesn't look like a Florian. I picture long hair and bulging muscles. Maybe somebody French."

"Yeah, well, laugh all you want, but Florian will get this done. I guarantee it."

19

LILITH

I called my best friend, Emily, for the first time since I'd met Liam. I was glad long-distance calling wasn't a thing anymore, because I was sure making a call to Paris would have probably cost a fortune otherwise.

I was sitting in the window nook of Liam's apartment with New York City sprawled out beneath me. With my forehead on the glass, I felt like I was floating above it all. Liam was at work, and I had the day off because William bought one of those water-powered jetpacks the other day and hadn't been able to stop playing with it long enough to come to work.

Emily picked up after a few rings.

"Lilith!" She said. "It has been killing me not to call you, but I know better than to pester you. Kinda like how a cat will only come sit on your lap if you ignore it, but if you call for it, it ignores *you*."

I smiled. I'd been doing that more lately, and I wasn't quite sure how to feel about it. "I like when you compare me to cats."

"I know," she said, and I could hear the smile in her voice. "Oh, I have good news. I am going to have one of my sculptures on display at the *Louvre*. It's going to be temporary, obviously, but they do this thing for students where you get to have a piece up in a student gallery for the weekend."

"Does the sculpture have a penis?"

She laughed. "Um, well. It's more like a city on a cloud kind of thing? It's hard to explain, but I'll send you pictures when it's up."

"Are you allowed to do something actually cool like that? I thought modern art was just spilling paint on random objects that aren't traditionally used as canvases. Well, that, or slapping a really graphic depiction of penises and vaginas on things because it's edgy."

She didn't say anything for a few seconds. "Hey... You sound different."

"What? No I don't. Probably just your shitty phone."

"No. You sound happy. What's going on over there? Did you watch somebody die recently?"

"It's a guy," I said slowly. "Like a relationship, I guess you could call it."

Another pause.

"Lilith!" She squealed.

I pulled my ear away from the phone and winced at the sudden burst of sound. "Don't get all weird on me. Okay?"

"Okay. *Okay.*" Emily blew out a slow breath like she was actively trying to calm herself. "How long?"

"A month," I said. "I've been living in his place now for like three weeks. Roosevelt is here, too."

"What's his name?"

"Liam."

"Wait, you moved in with him after a week? That seems fast. He's not some kind of weirdo, right?"

"It's just temporary. The move-in. I mean, my apartment is basically empty now and I haven't been over there in over a week... but I never promised him I'd be staying long term."

"Okay, so you moved in after a week. Temporarily. You're obviously falling pretty hard for him, but you're also trying to hold back from committing because..."

"I'm not holding back from committing. I'm just, I don't know, waiting? I've never done this before. High school relationships were easier because moving in wasn't an option. You just sat next to the guy on the bus and ate with him at lunch. Done deal. Now I'm supposed to figure out what everything means?"

Emily laughed. "Okay. Look. Obviously, I'm no expert, either, but if you moved in, it's pretty serious. There's a natural progression. Boyfriend, move-in, engagement, marriage, kids. You could mix up the order if you wanted, but that's kind of the basic formula."

"By your formula, I should be expecting an engagement ring any day now."

"Why don't you sound as horrified by that idea as the Lilith I know and love?"

"He's not going to propose. Besides, it's all complicated. He's got an evil step-sister and we've got this plot for revenge that is still panning out. So everything is kind of on hold until we figure out if we've sabotaged her life enough to stop worrying that she's going to come after us."

Another pause.

"It makes a little more sense now. For a guy to interest you, it would have to involve some weird, screwed up stuff like that." She laughed. "I can totally picture you scheming to ruin some poor woman's life."

"Yeah, whatever." I was smiling again, mostly because I was thinking about the fun I'd had sneaking around with Liam to try to keep tabs on Florian and Celia. William had let us hold on to his spy gear, and snooping had become one of our go-to evening time-killers. Of course, our version of snooping was more like parking in a car somewhere we thought they'd go, getting distracted talking for an hour, and then calling it a night with cheap takeout and a movie back at his apartment.

Our only sightings of the couple had been once or twice on the way into a store together. Considering we'd spent hours together under the pretense of spying on them, it was pretty clear what our real motivations were by now.

"So, any Christmas plans? Ryan and I were thinking of coming back home for the holidays. Just to see everybody. It has been forever."

"If thirteen months is forever, then yes, it has."

"You can be so literal sometimes."

"To answer your question, no. I haven't really figured out what we're doing for Christmas yet. I don't know what to get Liam, either. I have a feeling he probably bought everything he ever wanted, so I'd kind of need to get all sentimental to get him something nice."

"I have an idea..."

LIAM AND I WERE SITTING IN A CROWDED COFFEE SHOP TOGETHER.

"Price said Florian hasn't been checking in with him anymore. Ignoring his texts and everything. Florian's also not digging into our funding nearly as hard as he was at the start."

"What do you think that means? Could Celia have dug the truth out of him?"

"It's possible. Or maybe he actually likes her?" Liam frowned at the idea and then shook his head like he'd just said something crazy. "That wouldn't make sense, though. It has to be something else."

"Price did say Florian was kind of a sociopath. I'd say your sister is, too."

"Step-sister. And yeah, but I just can't picture it. And even if they really were hitting it off, I'm sure it would turn ugly very fast when she found out he's not actually a billionaire. The guy makes decent money, but I doubt it's more than Walter. She'll still drop him to the curb as soon as she finds out."

"Yeah. I almost feel bad. What if he did fall for her and we're just setting them *both* up for heartbreak? I'm happy to ruin Celia's life, but this Florian guy was just doing us a favor."

"My Lilith feeling bad for somebody?" He reached across the table and put his hands to my forehead. "Are you feeling okay, babe?"

I bit my lip. He'd started using pet names for me a week or two ago, and even though I thought pet names were obnoxious and gross when I was single, I'd had a change of heart. Hearing them from Liam made my stomach flutter and my face flush, even if he called me something stupid like "chicken nugget" or "sweet cheeks." He liked to mix it up, but his standard seemed to be "babe," which held a kind of casual affection that I couldn't get enough of from him. "I feel great, actually."

"It's probably because you're actually eating like a normal human being now," he said, oblivious to what I actually meant. "I knew once we got your macronutrient balance in check, you'd feel like a million bucks. I'm honestly surprised you could walk and talk with as little protein as you were taking in. It was a miracle of science."

"Keep talking about macronutrients and I'm going to spontaneously die of boredom," I said.

He grinned. "Fine. As long as you keep eating what I cook for us, I'm happy, even if you won't let me talk about it."

I nodded. "That was the deal." Liam turned out to be a great cook. He had been appalled to learn that my diet was a steady rotation of Ramen noodles, macaroni and cheese, and pizza. As he put it, I was missing a third of the essential nutrients my body needed. *Apparently,* I was supposed to be eating protein and not just fats and carbs. Who knew. I wasn't about to admit it to him, but I had been feeling extra good ever since he started cooking for me. It had been a little harder to seem so cranky and sarcastic all the time, but that also could've been the new boyfriend effect.

He even had been considerate enough to simply work protein into the foods I already liked.

Now my ramen had beef in it, my macaroni and cheese had bacon, and my pizza wasn't just cheese. He'd also been slowly introducing me to some foods that he called "adult" food, which I found vaguely insulting. Then again, I could also admit my diet was pretty much still entirely made up of the things I'd learned to eat on the cheap in my college days. Luckily for him, his "adult food" was actually pretty tasty, so I didn't complain much, as long as he didn't get all nutrition dork on me and try to teach me the science behind it, that was.

"Can I admit something?" I asked.

"Yes, but I have something to admit too."

"Let's say it at the same time."

"Okay, on three," he agreed. "One, two, thr—"

"I don't even care about getting revenge on Celia anymore," I said.

"I am falling in love with you," he said.

We locked eyes, and the hum of conversation in the coffee shop seemed to dull in my ears. *I am falling in love with you.*

I opened my mouth to say something, but couldn't think of the right words, so I ended up just tearing off little pieces of my napkin and rubbing them through the ring left by my coffee cup. "So," I said finally. "I feel like mine was a little less groundbreaking, and I feel a little guilty for that."

"I agree," he said. "You should feel guilty."

I didn't look up, but I thought I could hear the grin in his voice.

"But," I added. "If you wanted to look deeply into what I said. You could make the argument that I wanted revenge against Celia so badly, and for me to stop caring as much about it must mean I started caring about something even more."

"Right. And given the size of your revenge boner you were always talking about, I can only assume that means your boner is now fueled by something else, and it's maybe even larger than it was before."

"You could possibly infer that."

"A love boner," he whispered.

I sputtered out a laugh, then bit my lip as I met his eyes again. I could see it there. Not just how he felt about me, but why I suddenly knew I loved him too. It was probably different for everybody, but for me, loving Liam wasn't just because we got along or because he made me laugh. It was because he'd found a way to bring out the best in me. Maybe that was selfish, but I think everyone is actually selfish on the inside, and what better reason is there to love someone than finding somebody who teaches you to love yourself?

"A love boner," I agreed.

"So what do we do about Celia?" he asked. "Just call the whole thing off?"

I frowned. "I don't know. I mean, I don't feel like I have to see her life ruined or anything, but it's not like I want to go buying her gift cards and cupcakes, either. What if we just kind of cut contact with this Florian guy and let him do whatever he wants?"

"Just walk away from it?"

"Yeah. Maybe it still ends in disaster for her. Maybe she finds true love. Who really cares?"

He laughed. "I have to admit, I still don't want her to get off this easy. I can back off the whole ruining her life thing, but we need to ruin *something*. At least her day. Maybe her week."

I laughed. "Now you sound like me."

He grinned. "Wait until you hear my plan."

20

CELIA

I made myself a cup of coffee and stared out the kitchen window. It was snowing, and for the first time in a long time, I felt happy. Florian and I were going to go golfing, which meant I had a reason to finally wear the adorable outfit I had for a golf outing. It was all designer, of course, and I didn't doubt the other wives and girlfriends would be glaring with envy.

I smiled and bit my lip. Life was good. Walter was due back home from a business trip in an hour, but he would let me get away with murder so long as I fluttered my eyelashes at him. He'd already met Florian a few times. I told him Florian was my personal trainer, and I'd simply say we were doing golf as a little exercise activity today when Florian came to pick me up. Walter would peck my cheek and wish me good luck.

Being with Florian had made life with Walter more repulsive. I thought of his dry, cracked lips and the soft, supple warmth of Florian's. I thought of how cold Walter's bony hands always were on me compared to the strong touch of Florian. The idea of divorce had crossed my mind more than once already, even though I knew the prenuptial agreement was ironclad. If I divorced Walter, I got nothing. Florian could take care of me, but the thought of walking away from Walter with nothing grated at me. I'd suffered years to wait for the day when he'd pass and leave everything to me. If I left, it would've all been for nothing.

Oh, well. I took one last sip of my coffee and remembered I hadn't checked the front door for packages yesterday. I stuck my head out and saw two boxes. One was a big, cardboard box from eBay. Probably some car part Walter had ordered, as usual. It would join the heap of unused parts that he dreamed of eventually using to piece back together his old project cars. The other box was more interesting. It was purple, sleek, and very girly.

I immediately thought of Florian. He must've sent it to me as a surprise. I left Walter's box outside and took the purple package inside. I sat on the couch and carefully unwrapped the bow to read the message on the card:

"Had this custom-made, just for you. Just press the little red button to get the party started. It will be unforgettable...

Best,

L and L."

I frowned down at the card. L and L? I wondered if it was some reference to a poem. Florian was exceptionally well-read, and he was always talking about books and things I'd never heard of. I put it from my head and opened the box.

It was a dildo.

I laughed, then bit my lip as a flush of warm excitement passed through me. *Florian, you dirty bastard.* It was bigger than any dildo I'd ever seen, and I felt oddly compelled to know what it would feel like. Besides, the small red button at the base of the thing had me absolutely curious. *Press the little red button to get the party started.* I figured it was to turn on the vibrator, but then why would he have had it custom made?

Ten minutes later, I had a few candles lit in the bedroom and I was ready.

I slid it inside and had to catch my breath. It *was* big. Almost too big. For a second, I nearly gave up, but knowing Florian, he'd ask how it went, and I didn't want to disappoint him. I kept trying until I had it inside me, and then I reached for the little red button.

I pressed it and braced myself for the vibrations. Instead of vibrations, I heard a strange sound that took me a second to place. It was a phone ringing from what must have been a speaker inside the dildo. *What the hell?*

"911, what's your emergency?"

"There's no emergency," I said quickly as I tried to pull the dildo out of me. In my panic, I must have been tense, because I couldn't get it out. I pressed the red button again, hoping it would hang up the call.

"Maam? Is everything okay?"

"It's fine!" I shouted. "I just can't figure out how to hang up the fucking dildo, okay?"

"I'm going to send a trooper, just to be safe."

"No, you idiot! I just--don't send anyone. I'm fine."

"Just stay on the line with me. Officers will be arriving in a few minutes."

I let loose every swear word I knew as I tried to get the stupid thing out of me, but it wouldn't budge. The more I panicked, the more it felt stuck. I spent a few minutes ignoring the woman on the phone as I dug out some lube and tried to ease it out of me, but still couldn't make any progress.

Then I heard a car door in the driveway. Keys rattled downstairs in the front door, and I heard footsteps coming up the stairs.

"Honey, I'm back! Where's my kiss?"

"*Fuck*," I muttered.

"Is everything okay, ma'am?" the voice blared from my crotch.

Now that Walter was home, I realized how incredibly loud the speakers in the dildo were.

"Shut up!" I hissed. "He'll hear you!"

I threw on a bathrobe and hurried out into the hallway as fast as I could with an oversized dildo stuck inside me.

"Hey," I said. I tried to sound casual and smooth, but there was a hitch in my voice.

Walter smiled and wrapped me in a hug. "Still in your bathrobe? That's not like you."

"Well, it has been a lazy morning."

We both turned toward the front of the house at the sound of police sirens and car doors opening and closing.

"What is that?" Walter asked.

"I'll get it. Don't over-exert yourself, honey." I kissed his cheek and smiled before limping down the stairs and toward the front door.

I opened the door before they could knock, sticking just my face out. Two burly officers were looking back at me with concerned looks on their faces.

"It's okay, officers. Just misdialed the number. I tried to tell the operator, but she wouldn't take the hint."

"It's my job to call the police in situations like this, Maam," chimed a voice from inside my vagina.

I clenched my legs together and felt my eyes widen.

The officers shot me puzzled looks.

"Where is that coming from?" asked one of them.

"It's a smart home," I said. "Speakers everywhere."

"It sounded like it was coming from *you*, ma'am. Is it okay if we come inside?"

"No," I said. "It's not okay. I'm perfectly fine here."

I wanted to pull my hair when I saw Florian's car come pulling into the driveway. He got out quickly and came rushing to the door at the sight of the cop car and the police.

"What's going on?" Walter asked from behind me. "Oh, hi, Florian," Walter said when he saw Florian come up the stairs beside the officers.

I felt like screaming. The dildo inside me had started

vibrating softly, but now it was getting more intense, and I was having trouble thinking straight. "Everybody should just go home, okay?"

The officers exchanged a look.

"Are you okay?" Florian asked.

"I'm fine!" I shouted. There was a gut-wrenching feeling as the weight of the dildo and the vibrations finally jarred it loose. The entire thing slid out of me and flopped to the ground between my legs where it was buzzing and rotating slowly on the ground.

"Should I dispatch another team of officers?" asked the dildo.

I pressed my palms to my eyes. In a flash of rage, I thought back to the card attached the package. L and L. Lilith and Liam. I knew it was them.

EPILOGUE

I'd never been a big Christmas guy in the past, but this year, I had someone to celebrate it with. Even though Lilith claimed she thought Christmas decorations were for "those dorks who wear ugly sweaters and go door to door caroling," she didn't complain when I came home with boxes of decorations to put up in the apartment.

William Chamberson was throwing a "Christmas Eve Bash" at his place, and he had invited us. After seeing his whipped cream birthday suit, I was admittedly a little reluctant about agreeing to go, but Lilith said her best friend and her husband were flying in from Paris to be there, so I couldn't say no.

We took an elevator up to William's apartment on Christmas Eve. Lilith was wearing a huge, grass-green sweater with a plush unicorn covered in glitter that was sewn to look like it was bursting out of her chest in Ridley Scott *Alien*-style.

"Weren't you the one talking about ugly Christmas sweater wearers like they were the plague just a week ago?" I asked. My own sweater was covered in LED lights and probably a fire hazard, but it fit the ugly bill too well to pass up.

"I'm wearing it ironically, so it doesn't count."

"Yeah, but everybody wears them ironically. So..."

"I'm making fun of the people who wear them ironically. It's *meta*. If you don't know what that means, you can ask Grammy."

I laughed. "The first thing I learned about Grammy was that you don't ask her questions. So no thanks. I'll just trust you on that."

I was surprised to see the party in William's apartment wasn't packed. I had expected hundreds of guests, but it looked like he'd instead opted for family and close friends.

Hailey, William's wife, was helping Bruce's wife, Natasha, move plates of food from the kitchen to a large dining room table. Grammy was sitting at the table next to an elderly, stooped man. William was in front of a huge wall-mounted TV and was wearing what looked like virtual reality goggles and holding controllers in both of his hands. Bruce was standing by with a bored look on his face as William excitedly described the game he was playing while swinging his arms around. From the looks of it, he was bashing and slashing at waves of caveman-like men in a gladiatorial arena in the game.

Lilith rolled her eyes at him. "He has been buying the dumbest stuff. He does this every Christmas. It's like he doesn't understand the concept, and he just starts buying whatever he can think of for himself for weeks leading up to Christmas."

"I understand the concept," William said, raising his voice from the living room. "But I also have impulse-control problems. There's a difference. Besides, I saved the biggest present for tomorrow morning. It's a baby elephant. I had to call in some favors, and I only get to keep it for a few weeks, but yeah. I get to have a baby elephant in my apartment—" he paused, ducking his whole body as he swung his arms around to fight off a group of men in his game. "Technically it's not exactly legal, but as long as nobody finds out, we'll be good."

Hailey paused at the table, eyes darting toward William. "A baby elephant?" she asked.

I expected her to start yelling at him, but she jumped up and covered her mouth as she let loose an excited squeal. "Oh my God. Seriously? Is it small enough to cuddle?"

"You can cuddle the *shit* out of it," William said. "I thought we could knit it some sweaters and stuff like that. Maybe little hats, but I don't know if they have enough of a head for a hat. Maybe trunk sweaters. That would be hilarious, right?"

Grammy sighed and nudged the man beside her. "You hear this, Earl? My grandson-in-law is why you don't give millions of dollars to idiots. Can you imagine the world if more people like him had money? We'd all be fucked."

Earl nodded, his cloudy eyes unfocused and distant. "You know," he said wheezily. "My parachute got caught in a tree on D-Day. I was stuck up there for three damn days before anybody cut me down."

Grammy looked at the ceiling and mouthed something. "Earl, you never fought in any wars. You have flat feet and you got out of the draft, you wheezing, old, wrinkled dick. The most interesting thing you've ever done is shit somebody else's pants, and that was *before* you were senile."

"I'm not senile. I just think you're sexy when you're worked up," Earl laughed as he coughed out a barking laugh.

Grammy grinned. "You're damn right I am."

Emily and Ryan arrived a few minutes after us. I expected them to be decked out in European-styled clothing, because almost everyone I'd ever known who spent more than a few weeks in Europe seemed to like coming back and making some kind of bold, obnoxious fashion statement. When I saw they were dressed relatively normal, I decided I already liked them.

Ryan shook my hand and smiled while Emily went to say hi to Lilith. "So you're the one who tamed Lilith, huh? You do look kind of capable," he said, sizing me up. "Still, I didn't think anyone could do it."

"Doubt they can. I didn't tame her. It's more of a give and take kind of thing."

"Makes sense. Sometimes I think that's how it is with Emily and me."

Ryan went off to talk to Hailey and Grammy a little while later, and I was surprised to see Lilith wrapping Emily in a tight hug. When they pulled away, Lilith's eyes even looked a little watery.

"I missed you and your stupid face," Lilith said.

Emily had full-blown tears in her eyes as she laughed. "If I'd known I just had to leave the country to get you to be so affectionate, I would've done it a long time ago."

"Yeah, well, don't get used to it," Lilith said. "Next time I might just poop on your pillow."

She glanced over at me and saw the horrified look on my face, then cracked a smile.

"Okay, yeah," Lilith said. "Out of context, I can see how that would be weird. It's a cat thing? Inside joke... Or maybe we can just pretend I never said it."

I grinned. "Not judging."

Eventually, Lilith wandered over toward the TV where William was playing his game. "That actually looks kind of cool. Can I try?"

Bruce looked relieved, and he took the opportunity to quietly back away.

William happily helped Lilith get the headset on and within minutes, she was snarling as she hacked off the heads and arms of poor, cartoon gladiators.

William nudged me. "She's a natural. It took me a few hours to get the hang of it."

"Yeah. It's kind of scary how good she is at dismembering people. I always thought all the stabbing stuff was just a joke."

"She does like to joke about stabbing people. Doesn't that

freak you out when you guys fight? You know? I'd be worried she was going to come after me in my sleep or something."

"We don't really fight, actually."

"Ah," William said, nodding wisely. "You should try it. It's more fun when there are fights. Makeup sex and all that. She *does* do sex, right?"

"I can hear you," Lilith growled. "And don't answer that, Liam, or we'll have our first fight."

ON CHRISTMAS DAY, LILITH AND I DECIDED TO HAVE OUR OWN celebration. I thought long and hard about giving her an engagement ring as a present, but I decided it didn't matter how ready I was. What mattered was her. For all her joking with Emily, Lilith really was like a cat. If I pushed too hard and too soon, I worried I could scare her off. So instead of wrapping the ring I'd bought and giving it to her, I promised myself I'd wait. At least for another month, even if it would still be fast by all normal standards. Part of me wanted to let her finish her classes for business school so I could combine the proposal with the start of her new career, but I didn't think I'd be able to wait that long.

The weather was perfectly cooperative and we woke to a view of New York City coated in a soft blanket of powdery white snow. From sixty floors up, we couldn't hear the honking horns or feel the frustration of those down below trying to drive their way through the snow. Instead, we had the picture-perfect view and the soft sound of Christmas music playing across the sound system.

Lilith was wearing the PJ's I'd given her, which were covered in a print of Santa wearing a biker-themed suit and riding motorcycles, along with some depictions of him blowing things up with grenades and machine guns. Little by little, Lilith was smiling more and seemed less afraid to be happy in front of me, but I still knew she preferred irony over sincerity more days than not.

"I'm going to admit it," she said as we sat down in front of the tree with warm cups of coffee. "This is the most perfect Christmas I've ever seen. This would totally be like a scene from some Christmas commercial or Hallmark movie."

"And does my dark, sarcastic Lilith feel like she's trapped in a nightmare because of it?"

"No. Not at all." She gave me a crooked smile, clutching her cup from under her baggy sleeves where only her fingertips were visible. "I feel like I have permission to enjoy this, if that even makes sense. Like you taught me to give myself permission, I guess?"

"I'll accept the credit."

She chewed her lip and stood to grab a small package from under the tree. It was in a purple box that looked suspiciously familiar to the one that had been put in my mailbox by mistake a month ago—the one that had in many ways been the spark to start everything between us. "This is for you," she said. "I got you some other stuff, but this one is kind of the doozey."

"You got me a dildo? You shouldn't have... Like, seriously. I'm not going to judge, but I really don't have any desire to use this on myself, so—"

"Open the package, you idiot."

I smirked, then pulled at the bow. I felt my eyebrows squeeze together when I saw what was inside.

A pregnancy test. A positive one.

"That shouldn't be possible," I said quietly. "We've used protection."

"Apparently you have highly determined sperm, because this is the fourth one I took, and they all say the same thing."

"This is yours?"

"No," she said dryly. "I stole a pregnant ladies piss, splashed it on this, and thought it'd be a cool Christmas present. *Yes*, it's mine, and you had better start talking about how excited you are soon or I'm going to get self-conscious."

I sat back on the couch, looking down at the test with a stunned look on my face. "A baby?" I asked.

"Yes. Sex causes pregnancy. Then pregnancy causes babies. If you're still trying to figure it out, babies are those little, hairless things that turn into people."

I reached out and pulled her in to hug her. "I didn't know I wanted a baby until right now," I said into her shoulder.

She slid her arms around me and laughed. "Well, that's good. Because you're getting one, whether you want it or not."

"I do," I said. The words sparked something in me, and I pulled back from the hug, deciding suddenly that it wasn't too soon.

I got off the couch and got on one knee, pulling the ring from my back pocket. "Sorry, I didn't wrap it, but I was trying to wait so I didn't scare you off. Now it looks like you're stuck with me, so do you want to make it official?"

"That's so romantic," she laughed, bit she was smiling down at the ring. "I do."

I slid it on her finger and stood back up to kiss her. Lilith wasn't one for long, gushy hugs, but she didn't complain when I held her tight and didn't let go. I wanted to capture the moment and remember it just as it was, and her sarcastic ass could deal with it.

When I finally let her go, I remembered what I'd been waiting to tell her all day. "Since we're doing good news," I said. "I got a text from Florian this morning."

"What, she's going to sue us over the dildo?"

I laughed. "She hasn't so much as sent me a passive-aggressive text since the dildo incident. I'm pretty sure we finally showed her we weren't afraid to hit her back where it hurts."

"I just wish Florian was still an inside man so we had more than the stolen police report to go off of. Although the line, "fell out of the subjects vagina with a resounding thump" makes me think the scene was dramatic enough to leave an impression on the officer. So we do have that."

"We do. And now we have this. Florian is eloping with Celia. He came clean about the plan and about not really being a millionaire. She didn't care, She actually loves him, at least as far as he can tell, and he says he loves her."

Lilith looked at me like my eyes had fallen out of their sockets. "You're serious?"

"Yes," I laughed. "It wasn't the plan, but, yeah. Instead of ruining her life, we apparently played matchmaker and did a damn good job. The only loser is Walter. I don't even know if he has found out that she's gone yet."

"Walter was a dick. I looked up his track record when I was feeling guilty one night. It was a bunch of stuff about scandals and bribes. None of it completely stuck, but it seemed pretty clear he wasn't a clean shooter."

"Good. Then we can call this a total win, right? Celia finds the love of her life and probably won't be a bitter, crazed maniac for the foreseeable future, which means she'll probably leave us alone. Florian found someone equally sociopathic to be his match. It's perfect."

"Yeah," she said, eyes falling to my lips where she traced their outline with her finger. "Perfect."

PLEASE DON'T FORGET TO LEAVE A REVIEW!

Thank you so much for reading! Whether you loved the book or not, it would mean the world to me if you left an honest review on Amazon. I read every single review and take them all to heart, even on older books, so it's not just a great way to give me your feedback and help me improve, it's also one of the best ways to support me and help me find new readers.

If the books in this series are the first you've read by me, most of my other work generally has less humor. I still slide moments in here and there, but these books have been a much-needed mental break for me where I can write about something that's not as heavy while I get over some of the frustrating things I've been dealing with in the real world.

Hope you loved it!

P.S. I'm still deciding if there will be more books in this series. I'm going to let the reader response guide me one way or the other, so let me know if you want more!

xx

Penelope

WANT BRUCE AND NATASHA'S STORY?

If you found this book before Bruce's story, no worries! I tried my best to write them to be read in any order. You can find it here:

H
I
S
Banana

PENELOPE BLOOM

My new boss likes rules, but there's one nobody dares to break...

No touching his banana.

Seriously. The guy is like a potassium addict.

Of course, I touched it.

If you want to get technical, I actually put it in my mouth.

I chewed it up, too... I even swallowed.

I know. Bad, bad, girl.

Then I saw him, and believe it or not, choking on a guy's banana does not make the best first impression.

I should backtrack a little here. Before I ever touched a billionaire's banana, I got my first real assignment as a business reporter. This wasn't the same old bottom-of-the-barrel assignment I always got. I wasn't going to interview a garbage man about his favorite routes or write a piece on how picking up dog poop from people's yards is the next big thing.

Nope. None of the above, thank you very much.

This was my big break. My chance to prove I wasn't a bumbling, clumsy, accident-prone walking disaster. I was infiltrating Galleon Enterprises to follow up on suspicions of corruption.

Cue the James Bond music.

I could do this. All I had to do was land the position as an intern and nail my interview with Bruce Chamberson.

Forget the fact that he looked like somebody carved him out of liquid female desire, then sprinkled on some "makes men question their sexuality" for good measure. I needed to make this work. No accidents. No disasters. No clumsiness. All I needed to do was hold it together for less than an hour.

Fast forward to the conference room before the interview, and that's where you would find me with a banana in my hand. A banana that literally had his name on it in big, black sharpie. It was a few seconds later when he walked in and caught me yellow-handed. A few seconds after that was when he hired me.

Yeah. I know. It didn't seem like a good sign to me, either.

Get His Banana (Click Here!)

WANT WILLIAM AND HAILEY'S STORY?

William and Hailey's story can be found in Her Cherry (#5 Bestseller on Amazon and Wall Street Journal Bestseller!).

How'd I meet her?
Well, a gentleman never brags.
Thankfully, I'm no gentleman.
First, I paid for her cherry (pie, but that's not the point),

Next, I deflowered her.

After that? I left my business card and walked out like I owned the place.

Yeah, you could say we hit it off.

Hailey

How did I meet William?

He walked into my bakery, bought a cherry pie, stole a vase of flowers—I still have no idea what he wanted with them—and left his business card.

Before I say what I did with the business card, I should clarify something:

William couldn't have walked into my life at a worse time.

My bakery was failing.

My creepy ex refused to leave me alone.

Oh, and I was a twenty-five-year-old virgin, a fact my friends refused to stop hassling me about.

Fixing my little virginity problem with William would be like swatting a fly with a hammer. Overkill, but the best kind.

William was stupid hot, the kind of hot that makes women do stupid things. The kind of hot that made me think *crazy* things. Like thinking the fly wouldn't even mind getting hammered by William and his washboard abs. That makes two of us.

So I called him.

Maybe it was against my better judgment. Maybe I was stepping into a disaster waiting to happen.

I knew I was in trouble when he chuckled in that deep, sexy voice of his over the phone and said, "I'm still craving your cherry. Do you deliver?"

Get Her Cherry (Click Here!)

WANT RYAN AND EMILY'S STORY?

Don't miss His Treat, the latest addition to the Objects of Attraction series.

Having a hot boss isn't complicated or confusing at all,

Said no one ever...

But all I have to do is resist for a few months.

Come January, I'm flying to Paris to chase my dream of being an artist,

Too bad I can't have my *treat* and eat it, too.

I forgot to mention... My hot boss was also my high school crush.

Sort of.

First, I wanted to crush him with gooey affection.

In the end, I just plain wanted to crush him.

Now he's back, and he might as well have "do not touch" printed on his chest.

One tiny question: would it count if I didn't use my hands?

Let me answer my own question. *Yes, Emily, you raging horndog, it counts.* Besides, my dream is practically waiting for me like a perfectly wrapped, shiny little package if I can just behave. I'd be an absolute idiot to risk that, and I have a long, proud history of *not* being an idiot to protect.

Unless it's kind of like when you do really well in class all semester so you can afford to flunk a test at the end. Three months *is* a long time, and if he's the one giving me the big, fat, dirty "F", it *does* add a little dose of temptation to the equation.

But all I have to do is one quick job for him. A few posters and a few props for a big Halloween party that he's hosting.

Then I just walk away from his dreamboat eyes and perfect body, grab a plane, and forget about all the beautiful children we could've squeezed inside our white picket fence.

Get His Treat on Amazon, (Click here!)

ROMANTIC COMEDIES

LAUGH OUT LOUD
-HIS BANANA
-HER CHERRY
-HIS TREAT
-HIS PACKAGE

LIGHTER HUMOR
-SINGLE DAD NEXT DOOR
-SINGLE DAD'S VIRGIN
-SINGLE DAD'S HOSTAGE
-THE DOM'S VIRGIN
-THE BODYGUARD
-MISS MATCHMAKER

MAFIA

START HERE
HIS

-MINE
-DARK
-BABY FOR THE BEAST
-BABY FOR THE BRUTE

BDSM

START HERE
KNOCKED UP BY THE
DOM

-KNOCKED UP BY THE MASTER
-KNOCKED UP AND PUNISHED
-THE DOM'S VIRGIN
-THE DOM'S BRIDE
-PUNISHED

Don't know where to start? I hope this helps! You can also check the next page for a more detailed guide on which of my books might be best for you. Otherwise, click this image to go straight to my catalog on Amazon and start browsing.

Continue for a more detailed reading Guide ——>

I have written more or less in three distinct styles since I started two years ago. This is a more detailed breakdown of how to find which of my books might suit your interest the most:

Laugh out loud funny:

His Banana: It's not so funny that it leaves sexy and steamy by the wayside, but there are several moments that should have you laughing out loud.

Lighter Humor:

I won't go into every book here, because no one would read all that, but these books don't focus as much on silly situations. There's more emphasis on the drama of the relationship and all the usual things you've come to know and love in a romance. However, I generally think it's safe to say that you'll find comic relief in a few situations, as well as with many of the side characters in these books.

Single Dad Next Door: Mechanic gets a new neighbor, and it just so happens he needs a wife if he wants to keep his grandfather's shop. The only problem is he hates his new neighbor.

This is the book I'd recommend starting with to get a taste for my lighter romantic comedies. It has one of my all-time favorite scenes that I still smile to think about. It was also the first romantic comedy I wrote, and if you're like me, it's fun to read through an author's catalog chronologically so you can watch them grow.

Mafia:

I've done two styles of Mafia books in my career. The first series (the Citrione Crime Family) is violent, punchy, sexy, and pretty in-your-face. The men are alpha and there's kidnapping, gunfights, and all kinds of drama. If you enjoy a side of action with your romance, my debut novel, "His" is the best place to start.

If you like the mafia to be more in the background than the foreground of the story, and you don't enjoy all the violence and physical action, "Baby for the Beast" and "Baby for the Brute" are the two books for you. These spend more time focusing on the development of the relationship, but the mafia aspect still weaves itself into the story, just not in a violent sense.

BDSM:

Just like mafia, I've done a couple styles of BDSM books. One universal in my BDSM books was my goal of writing BDSM for people (like me) who are kind of put off by all the extreme elements of the kink. Everything is consensual, the Dom's are responsible (with the exception of forgetting a condom here and there for story purposes *wink*) and all the tools and toys used are light and cause no serious harm.

My most popular book across all categories by far was Knocked Up by the Dom. It's the book that ended up on the USA Today Bestseller list. If you like all the background plot to be out of the way and you want a spotlight shining right on the relationship, this is the book for you. It also comes out of the gate very very steamy and doesn't let up. The three "Knocked Up" books are probably the most smutty books in my catalog.

My BDSM books outside the Knocked Up series have a much lighter tone. The Dom's Virgin is a good place to start if you like romantic comedy and BDSM. If you feel like reading something completely different than anything you've likely read in romance, you can also check out Punished by the Prince (kind of a fantasy/BDSM/royalty/romance mashup with action and world-building).

Enemies to Lovers:

This is a category that, like the laugh out loud books, I plan to add more to this year. If you don't want the dislike between the hero and heroine to be mostly superficial, give these books a try. They tend to be longer than my usual books and you may have to give the hero a chance before you warm up to them, but if I do my job, you'll end up loving them in the end!

Savage: Currently, this is my only published enemies to lovers book, but I'm confident it's one you'll enjoy. I also wrote a book called Hate at First Sight, but it won't be live on Amazon until around February, and it might have a different title by then. Keep an eye out for it though, I think it's a truly powerful book and maybe the best I've ever written. I can't wait to share it with everyone!

ALSO BY PENELOPE BLOOM

My Most Recent Books

His Treat (Top 6 Best Seller)

Her Cherry (Top 5 Best Seller and 4 weeks on the Amazon most sold list!)

His Banana (top 8 Best Seller and 3 weeks on the Amazon most sold list!)

Baby for the Beast (#60 Best Seller)

Baby for the Brute (We don't have to talk about rank on this one, do we?)

Savage (#20 Best Seller)

The Dom's Bride (#40 Best Seller)

(Babies for the Doms)

Knocked Up and Punished (top 21 Best Seller)

Knocked Up by the Master (top 12 Best Seller)

Knocked Up by the Dom (USA Today Bestselling Novel and #8 ranked Bestseller)

∾

(The Citrione Crime Family)
    His (Book 1)
    Mine (Book 2)
    Dark (Book 3)

∾

Punished (top 40 Best Seller)
    Single Dad Next Door (top 12 Best Seller)
    The Dom's Virgin (top 22 Best Seller)
    Punished by the Prince (top 28 Best Seller)
    Single Dad's Virgin (top 10 Best Seller)
    Single Dad's Hostage (top 40 Best Seller)
    The Bodyguard
    Miss Matchmaker

JOIN MY MAILING LIST

Join my mailing list and I'll email you about once a month when I have a new release. I don't do any cross promotion or filler emails. It's strictly a convenient way for you to get a head's up when my books are live, and I'll squeeze as many updates into the new release email as I can to let you know what's going on with me and my upcoming work.

Check out my website for my occasional blog posts and more

behind-the-scenes information about me, my books, and the author world than you'll know what to do with!

You can also find me on Facebook. It's usually the first place I'll post teasers for upcoming books and share anything important going on with me and my books.